TO BE SOMEONE 2

TO DAVE ENJOY
ALL THE BEST
Peter Meadows

PETER MEADOWS

VIVLIA

First Edition
First published in Great Britain in 2013 by
Vivlia Limited
7a Eldon Way
Eldon Way Industrial Estate
Hockley
Essex
SS5 4AD

Printed in Great Britain by
4edge Limited
www.4edge.co.uk

A catalogue record for this book is available from
The British Library.
ISBN 978-1-909833-06-7

Thanks to my lovely wife Nikki for her help and support over the last three years, and thanks to Pete Townshend for creating the character Jimmy and allowing me to continue his life.

Contents

PREFACE

In part one of Jimmy's turbulent life it almost seemed to have the perfect fairytale ending for him and his clique, or so he thought. But when you get one over on London's most notorious gangsters, Mike Warren, there can be some very worrying repercussions. Mike's death left a bitter taste in the mouths of London's underworld. A heavy threat lay in the polluted air over London by no other than Mike's daughter hell bent on the ultimate revenge.

From Jimmy's humble beginnings as a sharp pill popping Mod from Shepherds Bush, London to a respected(ish) night club owner but as always it comes at a price. As his life takes pace with all the glamour of a club hammer, this story brings on a whole new dimension to sex, drugs and rock 'n' roll. An explosive account of his onward, chaotic journey through the world of illicit deals, dodgy imports, gangsters, hookers and even murder which only adds unwanted heat to the already bubbling cauldron.

Jimmy manages to scrape through some of the most unimaginable situations and still makes it into his sixth decade albeit by the skin of his teeth and let's not forget, this is no run of the mill ticket, this is a man who believed in himself no matter what shit was thrown at him, a survivor, a person that stayed true to his roots and thrived to be someone .... and succeeded!

By Wolfy the Mod

CHAPTER 1

THE PUNCH BOWL

'Appy endings, we all love 'em. Snow White and Cinderella got their prince, Red Riding Hood was saved by the woodsman, Mowgli managed to avoid getting eaten by Shere Khan the tiger, then went on to meet some bird from the village. Yeah, you can't beat a happy ending, but life ain't always like that. I mean look at the poor old gingerbread man; he thought he was a clever little fucker, dodging all them animals that wanted to eat him and granted, for a biscuit, he was fucking quick. He'd wind the animals up, then run down the road singing "Run! Run, as fast as you can! You can't catch me! I'm the gingerbread man"! Well he met his match with the fox. The fox didn't 'ave to chase him; nah, he just led him into a false sense of security and when the gingerbread man trusted him he tossed him in the air, caught him, then fucking ate him.

I could quite easily have ended up just like the gingerbread man as I've met my fair share of foxes, so fuck knows how I've managed to survive. Sometimes I wish I'd been like that little girl in the Wizard of Oz – I must have watched it a hundred times but I can't think of her poxy name – anyway, I wish that I could wake up like her and my whole life could have just been one big fucking nightmare.

People look at me in my club getting pissed, 'aving a laugh, riding round town on my scooter like I ain't got a care in the world and they think I'm a lucky bastard, and yeah, I agree I've got a great life, but they don't know the sacrifices I've had to make along the way. Eight years in the nick then, when I got out, spending the next twenty years living with the threat of Mike Warren (the nastiest bastard gangster of all time) hanging over me. I can't tell yer what that done to me: not knowing one day to the next whether everything was gonna come crashing down and I'd lose the fucking lot and end up back inside. Thankfully that threat has been lifted now Mike's pushing up the daisies, but one thing I've learnt is not to take fuck all for granted. I'm well aware that with the circle of mates I knock about with, anything could 'appen.

Yep, life is sweet and The Punch Bowl is doing great. The partnership with Roger and Vinny was a fucking nightmare to begin with 'coz we all had different ideas on what makes a great night. At one point I just felt like saying "fuck it" and letting 'em get on with it. I mean it weren't like I needed the money – the bike shop was doing well now that Ken had sorted his gambling addiction out. It was Tracy that made me stick at it, and it was Tracy that came up with a great idea after she got pissed off with me bitching about the other two.

"Trace that's fucking it. I've 'ad enough. They can 'av the poxy club, tossers".

"What now"?

"We want different things; I want a sixties club, Vinny wants all that seventies disco shit and Roger wants to turn it into a fucking rave".

"So why should you be the one to walk away? If it weren't for you there wouldn't be a club".

"'Coz Roger can see where Vinny's coming from and Vinny can see where Roger's coming from, but they both think my idea's fucking stupid".

"They could have a point. You love your sixties, but it's not just about what you want".

"What you on about 'just what I want'? Everyone loves the sixties! You look at how packed the dance floor is when Tony whacks some Motown on".

"Yes. You're right, but do you honestly think you'd get away with it all night"?

"Yeah I do".

"It's simple then. There's three of you and there's three nights the club's open: you each have your own night".

"Trace, that's brilliant".

"I know".

Without doubt it was a great idea. That's what I love about Tracy. It doesn't matter what shit I'm in; she never lets it stress her, she just stays calm and manages to sort the problem out.

The next day I called a meeting with Vinny and Roger. Roger knew straight off that I had something to say.

"So Jim, what's on your mind"?

"Look, we all want different things for the club. I want my sixties, Vinny wants his seventies disco and dance music and you want a fucking rave. Fuck knows why at your age".

"Jim, I don't give a flying fuck what music it is, I'm not in this business to get my jollies like you. I'm in it for the money, simple as that and as much as you might like watching a load of old farts singing along to 'High Ho Silver fucking Lining', it don't bring the money in".

"He's got a point Jim", Vinny chimed in.

"Yeah I 'ave got a point and the shit you want ain't much better either".

Vinny ignored Roger and turned to me. "Jim, what's new mate? I ain't being funny, but I've got better things to do than go over this again and again".

"Well, Trace came up with a good idea. Why don't we 'ave a

night each"

"Great idea! I'm 'aving Saturday". Roger was first off the blocks, closely followed by Vinny.

"I'm 'aving Friday".

"Nah, bollocks! Why should I get the shittiest night"? I was fucking pissed at them.

"It ain't open to debate. I'm 'aving Saturday and that's that. I'm off", and with that, Roger swaggered out the door, scratchin' his arse.

"It makes sense Jim. No-one parties hard on a Thursday night".

I gave up. "Alright I'll take the Thursday".

So much for democracy and having the vote. As usual, Roger gets what Roger wants. We're equal partners, but Roger is the boss and he usually gets his own way, so I was just grateful I got at least one night to myself. Vinny was right anyway; no-one parties hard on a Thursday night 'coz of work the next day. I was struggling to come up with ideas on how to get people out on a Thursday so I sat down with Tracy.

"Right Trace, it's sorted. They went for it and we 'av a night each".

"What night you got then"?

"Well I thought I'd take the Thursday, Vinny Friday and Roger Saturday".

"Did yer bollocks, Roger decided, didn't he"?

"Yeah he did, but Thursday's alright".

"So when was the last time we went clubbing it on a Thursday then"?

"We don't".

"Exactly. We normally go to the pictures or up the West End to a show or a concert".

"That's right. We like to watch something so how about we put a sixties band on?"

"They'd have to be bloody good to play every Thursday; you

ain't gonna wanna watch the same band every week".

She was right, as much as I like live music, I couldn't watch the same set every week. Roger was right too, most people who love the sixties aren't piss-'ead party animals, so we had to come up with a night where if you wanna dance you can, or if you just wanna listen and watch you can. I spent ages trying to think of a way to please everyone and make it work before it finally came to me.

"I've got it! What's our favourite program that we never miss and always record"?

"The Rock and Roll Years".

"That's been on the box for years and the reason is that people love nostalgia. You've got great music plus all the old news footage and great times. That's what we need to recreate down the club".

"So you've gotta find a band that can cover the fifties, sixties and seventies".

"No, no we don't, we just need a fucking good sixties cover band who can cover the sixties. No, we get a fucking big screen behind the stage and while they're playing say, a number by *The Who*, you have footage of *The Who*".

"Sounds good".

Too right it sounded good. I'm not normally one for blowing smoke up my own arse, but it was a great idea. I was buzzing again so I started checking different bands out. There were lots of Soul bands doing all the old *Otis Redding*, *Eddie Floyd* and *Wilson Pickett* stuff, which was alright but not everyone's cup of tea. I needed a band that could do *The Who*, *The Kinks*, *The Yardbirds*, *Spencer Davis*, *The Small Faces*; all the stuff that I liked, but I was struggling. I had the screen and projectors sorted and the DJ was on board, but it wouldn't work unless I got the band.

A week later, I was starting to give up on the idea of having a resident band and had resigned myself to just putting a different one on each week, when we went to one of Tracy's friend's weddings. I weren't gonna go 'coz I hate weddings but Tracy's mate persuaded me by saying they'd booked a really good band. Now, my experience of wedding reception bands ain't good; they're usually old boys doing shit *Beatles* covers and *24 hours from Tulsa* kind of crap. While we were stuffing our faces, I was watching the band bringing their gear in and setting up. Shit, these guys had some serious gear; stacks of Marshall amps, an impressive mixing desk and, when they undid their guitar cases and pulled out Rickenbackers, they really started to stir my interest. The bride's dad went on for ages, then the best man, while out the corner of my eye I could see the band clipping on their guitars as if they were gonna rip into something while the best man was still boring the shit out of us with his relentless tales of what him and the groom did as kids. Then the best man said "That's enough from me, get pissed and enjoy The Overtures!", The lights all went off and the National Anthem played, which pricked the hairs on the back of my neck up. When the anthem stopped, the band ripped straight into 'I Can't Explain', 'You Really Got Me', 'Keep On Running' and 'Sha La La La Lee' then introduced themselves: "We're The Overtures, if anyone's got any requests we'll be glad to do 'em as long as they're from the sixties". I couldn't believe what I was seeing – they were exactly what I was looking for! It didn't matter what people asked for, they knew it.

"Do something by *The Searchers*", one bloke shouted out.

"What do you want? We know 'em all", the bass guitarist called back.

"'Needles and Pins!'" he shouted and almost immediately they were into it; they were like a live jukebox.

They played for about an hour before they took their break and the two guitarists went straight to the bar, so I approached the drummer.

"Alright mate? That was fucking amazing".

"Cheers. Glad you enjoyed it".

"You local are yer"?

"No, we're from Hoddesdon".

"I'm Jimmy".

"I'm Steve".

"I own the Punch Bowl and I've been looking for a band like yours to do a regular spot on a Thursday night... you interested"?

"Talk to Den, the bass player, he takes care of bookings". Den was still at the bar talking to some bird. I don't normally interrupt, but I knew they were only having a thirty minute break before their next set. As soon as there was a pause in their conversation I butted in.

"Den, sorry to butt in, but have you got a card with your number on? I'm interested in booking yer". The blonde bird he'd been talking to walked off as Den's eyes followed her all the way to the table.

"Very nice".

"Know her do yer"?

"No, she's just some bird who wants a request for her dad".

"What she want"?

"'Return to Sender'".

"You don't do that old crap do yer"? I was surprised.

"We do it all mate".

I'd heard that one before. I needed to know how serious these guys were. "You say all. Roughly how many"?

"We've got a repertoire of about three hundred tracks".

Woah! This was it. "Great, you're exactly what I've been looking for, I own The Punch Bowl and I was wondering if you would be interested in doing a residency on a Thursday night"?

"Always interested in work Jim. Give me a call tomorrow and we'll talk then; I don't like talking business while we're gigging. You got a favourite song you wanna hear"?

To be honest, they'd played most of my favourites so I thought

I'd test them and pick one of Tracy's favourites, "Yeah, can you do *Simon and Garfunkel*'s 'The Boxer'"?

"We'll give it a go".

"Can you play it for my wife Tracy"?

"No problem".

It certainly wasn't a problem, it was the first number of their second set and it was note perfect. The next day we met up to talk business and he agreed to fix the price for six months before reviewing it.

The first night went exceptionally well. We only had about sixty or seventy people in, but everyone had a great night and, to my surprise, I'd say three quarters of them were dancing. The band played everything from *The Who*, *Stones*, *Kinks*, *Small Faces,* and not just *Beatles* hits, but their obscure album tracks as well. The following week numbers were up to about a hundred and every week we were seeing the same faces along with the new. After six months, the place was packed out and, naturally, the band wanted more money so we upped the entry fee a bit. It was a great night. In the summer we opened up a big patio area and sold burgers. It was a really friendly atmosphere where all the regulars knew each other and there was no aggro. The best thing about it though, was that Roger and Vinny left me alone. Vinny was so impressed with my Thursday nights that he started putting on dance bands and ended up having a resident seventies disco cover band doing all that 'I Will Survive' rubbish.

The real worry was Roger. Roger's always been a worry to me 'coz he's got his fingers in one too many pies for my liking. I didn't know too much about the rave scene before Roger enlightened me. It started off illegally in old warehouses and barns in the middle of nowhere and drugs were one of the main ingredients for success. In the sixties it was blues and purple hearts, but now it was ecstasy. Roger was making a fortune and it weren't from drink 'coz all they drank was water. He persuaded me to go to one of his rave nights and I can tell yer it was fucking horrendous. The kids were drugged up to the eyeballs. It was like being at the National Gurning Championship with their faces all twisted and contorted, eyes bulging, dribbling, soaking wet with sweat, and every toilet was full of puke. Every one of them kids was popping 'E's. I mean, you had to 'coz you couldn't have stayed in there without 'em. The security could only do thirty minute stints or else they'd go insane with all the strobe lights and noise. A few kids died through popping 'E's, but Roger didn't give a fuck. He started hiring bigger venues like leisure centres and he tried to get me involved. I would have made shit loads of money, but for me it's never been just about the money. I ain't that flash and I ain't that materialistic. I don't drive a hundred grand Bentley like Roger; I still ride round town on my scooter.

Three years on and things couldn't get any better. Me and Tracy were still loved up and the kids were at an age where we could leave 'em and go out more. I only had to work one night a week – if you can call getting pissed and dancing all night work – and, on top of all that, we was doing really well with the bike shop.

CHAPTER 2

KEN

Jim's a great bloke. I ain't got a lot in common with him, but we've always got on really well. He likes looking flash in his suits and riding round on his stupid scooter, while I like nothing more than putting on my leather jacket, getting on my Triumph, and hitting the road. I had a 'ton ten' out of it the other day. A weedy little fucker like Jim would never have been able to hold on to it at that speed. Come to think of it, he probably wouldn't have even been able to kick it over, Jesus! I've seen him nearly blow a bollock trying to start that stupid scooter some mornings. Jim's always said "it ain't about the bikes; it's the people who ride 'em", but for me it *is* all about the bikes. I love 'em! I love ridin' 'em, fixin' 'em and sellin' 'em. It's a good job we ain't all the same – it would be a boring world if we were.

Jim's done well and he deserves it 'coz he's had a lot of shit to deal with and now he's reaping the rewards. I was a big part of some of that shit and I was amazed Jim gave me a second chance. To be honest, I think the only reason he did was because he was married to my sister and I was with his sister. I suppose the way Jim looked at it was that we've all fucked things up and made mistakes. Putting all the bike shop's tax money on a horse was so monumentally stupid that you've gotta laugh – especially as the horse dropped dead with a heart attack. It's not just that we're family, it's that we're mates.

Jim likes to surround himself with blokes like me – I don't mean hairy arse bikers – I mean blokes that are a bit edgy and unpredictable, not normal and boring. There's Dave, who runs one of the biggest escort agencies, Rudy, a retired drug dealer, Vinny, the son of one of the most feared gangsters, Roger, who still is a fucking gangster, although I wouldn't exactly class Roger as a mate. I think with Roger, it's more a case of keeping your friends close and your enemies closer. I've told Jim time and again to sell up his share of the club and cut his ties with Roger and Vinny, but he won't 'ave any of it. I don't know if it's because he gets off on people thinking he's a bit of a gangster or if he feels safe being in a gang type situation – a bit like when he was in prison:. Surround yourself with the bad guys and you'll be safe. I think something Roger said to him a long time ago has stuck in his mind. When Mike was about and Jim wanted out, Roger said "while you're in, you're safe". Jim lives in his little bubble where he thinks he's safe, but you take a psycho like Mike off the street and it's only a matter of time before someone will jump in his shoes. When Mike was about there was a gang or a firm or whatever you wanna call it. It was safety in numbers. When Mike died and the firm was split, not everyone was happy, least of all Mike's daughters and Mr big-shot, Ace Face Ray. Ace Face Ray was a nick-name that had stuck with him from the Mod days of the Sixties. Jim and Ray had always had a sort of love–hate relationship, but when Jack Warren kicked Ray out of The Ritzy and gave it to Jim, it was definitely a hate–hate relationship. Jim weren't stupid though, and he knew Ray was always there in the background, just waiting to jump back in. What Jim didn't know was that when he declined Roger's offer of getting involved with the raves, Ray didn't, and him and Roger were running the biggest drug ring in the South of England.

When I fucked up and nearly lost Jim the bike shop, I promised myself and Sarah I'd knock the drinking and gambling on the head, but what can I say? We all have our vices: Booze and gambling are mine. The booze weren't the problem though – I mean, I weren't a fucking alky – it was the gambling that was my demon. Sarah thought she could control it by taking charge of the money; she'd give me 20 quid a week for the horses, 20 fucking quid! I felt like a little kid getting pocket money, it was fucking degrading, that's what it was. The rows we used to 'ave 'coz one week I'd have a dead cert and I'd ask her for an extra tenner, but she wouldn't have none of it and you know what? Nine times out of ten I would have cleaned up. Addictions are terrible things, whether it's booze, drugs, gambling, food or any other of life's pleasures, being hooked on them is horrible. I think you've gotta stop it altogether. You can't just dip your toe in, no, it's either all or nothing. Sarah thought she was helping by allowing me to carry on gambling – she thought she could control it – but anyone who's hooked on anything knows you can't control it. All she was doing was teasing and frustrating me. An alky or druggie can't hide their addictions because there's too many tell-tale signs they're still hooked. To fuel my addiction was easy: I started skimming money from the bike shop. I'd give customers discounts if they paid cash and that way I didn't have to put it through the books. I thought I was well clever, but as usual Sarah was one step ahead of me, she got suspicious when the rows we used to have about me wanting more money stopped. She went through the bike shop books with a fine toothed-comb and noticed the profits were dipping. She couldn't prove anything though, so the crafty cow only went and got our boy Steve to work in the shop. Steve's a good lad but he's always been a bit of a mummy's boy due to the fact that I didn't come into his life until he was eight or nine. I tried to get him into bikes, but I didn't stand a chance 'coz back in '79 and '80, when you had the big Mod revival thing going on, he was fifteen and all his mates were Mods. The fact that his uncle Jim was a Mod as well definitely didn't help. You wouldn't think that a father and son's differing taste in music and fashion would create such a big wedge between us, but that's exactly what it done. Instead of bringing his mates home, he'd hang out at Jim's club 'coz he didn't want them to know his dad was a biker. His mates used to think he was a right cool fucker having an original Mod for an uncle who still rode round on a scooter. Jim loved telling them all about the crazy sixties; how him and his mates saw *The Who* at the Goldhawk club, and how they'd all go down to Brighton. Steve didn't know nothing about bikes, but a poxy scooter he could strip down and rebuild blindfolded, so he bought old scooters and restored 'em.

Well, Sarah's little plan worked a treat and my cash flow was well and truly stemmed, so I went back to my old ways and started borrowing again. I was doing alright; I weren't making a lot, but I always managed to keep my head just above water with big Steve the money lender. Big Steve was a right 'ard bastard in his day, but he was getting on a bit now and knocking on the door of retirement. He used to shit the life out of me, but I reckon I could take him now, so I weren't too worried when my debt to him started creeping up to the ten grand mark. His limit was twenty – he'd never let yer owe more than that. A few years back I got to that limit and I paid him back, so I was a bit surprised to see him when I got to ten grand. Thankfully he popped down the shop when Steven was out getting parts.

"Alright Ken how yer doing"?

"Alright. Not too bad. You know the score: win some loose some".

"Yeah, I know the score alright. Trouble is you ain't been winning too much lately… in fact, looking at your account with me, you've won fuck all".

"Yeah, I ain't had much luck lately, but you know I'm good for it, so what you worried about"?

"Worried? I'm not worried Ken, it's you that should be fucking worried 'coz you ain't getting any more and I want what you owe me paid in full by the end of the month".

"You're joking! How the fuck can I come up with ten grand in four weeks"?

"Not my problem".

"Yeah, well it *is* your fucking problem 'coz I ain't got it, so you'll 'ave to fucking wait".

"I'm not sure I like the tone of your voice, and your body language suggests you fancy your chances Ken, which I find very disappointing, especially as I've come down here to help you out".

"Help me out? How did yer work that one out"?

"Well, your attitude to me confirms the time is right".

"Right for what"?

"Retirement, Ken".

"Retirement"?

"Yep. Years ago you'd never talk to me like that and you're not the only one, so I'm spending the next four weeks getting as much as I can back and whatever is left I'm selling on".

"Selling on – how the fuck does that work?".

"Simple, if after four weeks, you still owe me ten grand, I sell that debt to another collector for six grand. That means I lose four, which I can live with because I'm a rich fucker. You, on the other hand, will not be able to live with that because the firm I'm selling onto are very *very* naughty. I'm giving you four weeks purely to ease my conscience, because trust me Ken, you *don't* wanna fuck around with these people".

Big Steve's visit had me more than a little worried 'coz I've seen how some of these fuckers work. There was no way I could come up with that kind of money in four weeks; the only way I could is if I went cap in hand to Jimmy, but then there'd be a good chance he'd tell Sarah. I couldn't take that chance so I decided to wait and see who or what I was up against. The four weeks came round pretty quick and all I'd managed to scrape together was five hundred quid. When, after six weeks, they still hadn't made contact, I decided to take the five hundred to the bookies and put the lot on a hot tip at the 3.30 at Doncaster. If it had won I would've cleared eleven grand.

It was a month later that they grabbed me – I was walking home from the boozer when a white transit pulled up and I was pulled roughly in through the side door. I'm not sure where I was taken 'coz there was no windows in the van. When we stopped and they got me out we were in an industrial unit filled with boxes of hi fis and TVs. In front of me there was two big geezers and a woman – a real hard-faced bitch – who looked familiar, but I couldn't place her. She sat behind a desk and introduced herself.

"Hello Ken, I'm Doreen and this is Liam and Tony". She paused, leaving an uncomfortable silence. I shuffled. "Right, we've brought you here to discuss your account and see if we can come to some sort of agreeable repayment plan". She didn't make eye contact, just flicked though some paperwork as she spoke.

"So Ken, you owe eleven thousand..."

"No love, ten fucking thousand", I interrupted – *big* mistake. Before she replied, Liam smacked me straight in the side of my head and, even though I was pissed, I tell yer it fucking hurt. Doreen cleared her throat.

"Shall we start again? Now listen Ken, let's not get off on the wrong foot, I'm a very reasonable lady and I want our business with each other to run as painlessly as possible for you". She was actually starting to sound quite nice and reasonable, so I smiled. She exploded in a fit of anger.

"You ever smile or call me 'love' again, you fat useless piece of shit, Tony will take your fucking knee caps out".

Then, without warning, Tony flicked out one of those extendable coshes the old bill carry and smashed the back of my knee. I hit the floor like a sack of shit. Liam and Tony picked me up and sat me in a chair opposite Doreen.

"You seem to think you only owe me ten thousand".

"Yeah that's what I owed Big Steve".

"That's right, but that was six weeks ago. You haven't added the ten per cent interest that I charge per month".

"ten per cent"?

"ten per cent, Ken, so next month you'll owe me twelve thousand, one hundered".

"There's no way I can come up with that kind of cash".

"I do hate a defeatist attitude, there's always a way, let's start with your house – do you own it"?

"The house, the car, everything – it's all in my wife's name".

"And the bike shop? That's Jimmy's isn't it"?

"Yeah that's right. How did you know that"?

"I know a lot Ken. You'll be surprised what I know. Now tell me the set up at the shop. I want to know it all".

"Well, it's a bike shop. We sell and repair bikes and sell parts".

"Who's the young lad that started a while back"?

"That's my son, Steven, who sells the scooters".

Liam seemed interested at this point and piped up, "scooters? I didn't think they made 'em anymore".

I had to correct him: "They still make Vespas, but Steve buys in old Lambrettas from India and does 'em up".

"Interesting... so Jimmy's nephew imports scooters from India..." Doreen was fascinated.

"What's so fucking interesting 'bout that"? My question was followed by another smack in the side of the head from Liam.
"I ask the questions". Doreen replied sharply, before switching to sickly sweet. "Well it's been nice getting to know you Ken. You know the terms of our agreement now, so I look forward to seeing you in four weeks time".

I was put back in the van and dropped off back where they picked me up. I couldn't put my finger on it but something weren't right. I've come across a lot of money lenders and I know people who've owed a lot more than ten grand, but I've never seen anyone get that heavy so soon. This Doreen bird fucking hated me. I wondered how she knew about Jimmy owning the bike shop, and why she made a point of saying Steven was Jimmy's nephew. No, something weren't right and I knew I had to get her off my back. I had no choice but to sell my prized possession – my Vincent bike. It was worth at least fifteen grand, so I could pay her off and have a few grand to try and win some back.

Four weeks later and it was the same story. I was walking back from the boozer this time and this white van pulled up and I get dumped in the back. Only this time I'm not alone – there's another geezer in there.

"Alright mate you owe 'em a few bob as well"?

"Wish it was a few bob! It currently stands at forty grand. I'm Andy by the way".

"I'm Ken, fuck me I was worried about paying back ten".

"I never borrowed forty, only fifteen, but with their interest rates it soon gets out of hand..." He trailed off. "I don't know what happens now. I can't pay them and that's that".

"What did yer borrow the money for?"

"My life was shit; the missus left me, my business went bust 'cos of the recession, so I had this crazy idea of fucking off to Thailand and not coming back. You can live like a fucking king over there on fifteen grand".

"So why did yer come back"?

"'Coz I got fucking robbed! I lost the lot. How fucking unlucky can yer get"?

"Yeah that's shit luck alright. What do you know about this lot"?

"Not much, I borrowed from Big Steve".

"Yeah, so did I".

"I know one thing: They don't fuck about".

The van stopped and we got out in the same industrial unit as before. This time there was the two heavies, Tony and Liam, and a horrible little fucker who kept smiling. He looked a right nutter. Tony led me to the desk where Doreen was sitting and Liam led Andy to a big sheet of polythene and told him to kneel down. He sunk to his knees and Doreen said in a calm voice.

"So, Andy, have you got the funds to settle your account with me"?

"No. No I haven't".

"And if you can't pay me back, can you tell me what possible use you are to me"?

Before Andy had a chance to answer, the little creepy geezer strolled up behind him, put a gun to his head and blew his brains out. Literally, I've never seen so much blood and the smell was horrible. To say I was shitting myself is an understatement – it was like I was in a fucking gangster film. I was confused and shocked. What the fuck was going on? I shot a quick glance over to Doreen and she was lighting up a fag as if nothing had happened. She turned to the geezer with the gun saying

"Arthur, wrap him up and get rid of him".

He pulled the corners of the polythene up then gaffer-taped them together and dragged the body into another room. Doreen looked at me, smiled and asked

"Ken, what do you think of the way we dealt with Andy"?

"A bit fucking exteme". She just laughed.

"Andy was never going to pay that money back and he is of no possible use to me, so Arthur will now remove what's left of his head, along with his arms and legs, and dispose of him. Now *you* tell me Ken, have you got the funds to settle your account"?

"Not on me, no". I was trying to tread carefully, but the sweat was prickin' out under my armpits and I could feel my forehead getting hot.

"Andy was of no use to me".

"You never gave the poor fucker a chance to answer that"!

She sat there laughing while Tony and Liam joined in.

"Yes you're right, but we knew he was useless, whereas you can be very useful. In fact, so useful that I'm prepared to write your debt off; you won't owe me a penny".

"How can I be of use to you"? Not being in debt to these frightening fuckers sounded good to me. I was willing to do anything.

"Yes, it's surprising how a fat, disgusting biker with a gambling problem can be of use to anyone, but you can and, as long as you're a good boy, you won't see or hear from us again".

"So what's the crack then? What do you want me to do"?

"You received a container from India six months ago full of broken scooters and parts, which was delivered to Felixstowe by Red Sea Shipping. When it cleared customs it was taken to Unit 16 Botany Bay Trading Estate in Stevenage where a number of scooter dealers picked up parts that had been ordered".

"Well you know a lot more than me 'cos Steven deals with that side of things".

"From now on you'll be taking a healthy interest in all things related to importing from India. All the details are here in this envelope: contacts, cargo company, times, places; the lot".

"I don't get it".

"There's nothing to get. Just follow the instructions and you'll be alright. You fuck things up, you'll be of no use to me, and you know what happens to useless people, don't you"? I winced, thinking of Andy, the poor fucker. "Now, Tony will take you back and I never want to clap eyes on you again. Is that clear? Oh, and this meeting never happened".

I was dropped back dazed, shocked and confused, a hundred thoughts racing round my head. One of them was thank fuck I ain't gotta sell my bike now. How twisted is that? I've just witnessed some poor fucker get his brains blown out and I'm thinking about a fucking motor bike. Nothing added up, nothing made sense. Money-lenders don't go around blowing people's heads off who owe them money; they'd never get away with it, so poor Andy must have been a message to me that these people don't fuck about. I still couldn't place that bird Doreen, but she reminded me of someone, and it gave me a funny feeling I didn't know what was coming in that container from India, but it must be worth a bit for her to write off the twelve grand I owed.

I took the day off work to try and get my head round it. The envelope contained details of the previous container we'd had and the one that was coming in eight weeks' time. There was also a direct phone number to India for a bloke called Raj. The instructions were pretty clear. All I had to do now was convince Steve that my new interest in scooters was genuine 'cos I didn't want him linked to that container in any way. I waited a few days before I spoke to Steve because, to be honest, I was still in shock.

"Steve, how you getting on with doing them scooters up"?

"Alright, not too bad 'cos there's no shortage of spares and there's plenty of old ones about, thousands in India".

"Yeah, what was the deal on that last container you got"? I was trying to be casual.

"Well, to keep the cost down I split it with two dealers from up North".

"Wouldn't it be better if you got a container to yourself, so you could sell on to them dealers and make more"?

"You're right, but if I can't sell 'em then I'm stuck; what am I gonna do with a container full of scooters? For one, we ain't got the space, and two, I couldn't do all of 'em up on my own".

"Well, I've been watching yer son and I have to say I'm impressed. I've given up trying to get you into bikes but I want to work with yer, so I've been scaling down the bike business and I'm gonna work with yer on the scooters. What do yer reckon"?

"You serious Dad"?

"Yeah definitely. I think we'd work well together".

"You'll be getting a parka next".

"I said I'd do 'em up with yer, not fucking ride round on 'em".

"Great"!

"Okay – you know more about scooters and the prats that ride round on 'em than I'll ever know, so you're better off selling 'em and dealing with the buyers, while I take care of the paperwork and buying in stock".

"We might as well deal with the same bloke I got the last lot from, he done us a good deal".

"A good deal? You're fucking joking. I saw the invoice for that container and straight away I could've saved four hundred quid on that alone".

"Fair enough. You deal with it then".

Well it weren't too hard convincing Steven. In fact, when I was talking to him about it I actually felt I was connecting with him properly for the first time.

"Right Steve, what exactly are we getting from India"?

"Lambrettas, GP200s. I've got a number in the office for a bloke called Singh who I've been dealing direct with".

"Any particular colour"?

"Nah. As long as they're runners, we strip 'em down and spray 'em to order".

"How many did you have from that last shipment"?

"Four".

"Is that all"?

"Well yeah. The demand ain't that great 'cos a lot of scooterists like doing 'em up themselves. Plus I've only got one pair of hands".

"Well I'm helping yer now, so we'll double the order plus we'll buy in another twenty and sell 'em on as projects".

"Where the fuck are we gonna store twenty-eight scooters"?

"I know someone who's got a half empty industrial unit".

"Singh will be well chuffed".

"Yeah looking at what he charged you for that last lot I bet he would. Nah, fuck Singh. Leave it with me and I'll sort it".

Steve done me a list of all the parts we needed along with the twenty-eight scooters. All I needed to do then was ring this Raj geezer in India.

"Hello is that Raj"?

"This is Raj".

"I'm Ken, from Jim's bike shop in England".

"Hello Mister Ken. I've been expecting your call. I need a list of all the parts you need and how many scooters you require".

"I've got the list 'ere, you got a pen"?

"No, Mister Ken. Fax the list over and I'll contact you when your order is on its way".

"What about payment"?

There was a pause before he answered. He laughed dementedly as he said, "Payment has been taken care of Mister Ken. Send me that list and I will be in contact with you shortly. Goodbye".

It was two weeks later that I got a fax through with an invoice for fifteen grand, which said paid in full at the bottom of it. I checked the prices against the previous invoice from India and it was a lot less. I couldn't believe my luck! I could now legitimately draw out fifteen grand from the bike shop's account, stash it somewhere and I was well sorted for the gee gees' for fucking ages. I knew something dodgy was going on, but I didn't understand why this Raj geezer got the hump because I said I'd sign the invoice. He insisted that Jimmy did it, so I forged the signature. I couldn't see what difference it made 'cos we weren't paying fuck all anyway.

A week later I got a fax telling me that the scooters had arrived and where to pick 'em up from. Like I said, I knew something was dodgy, so when I picked 'em up I went on my own. As soon as I walked through the door to the unit, I recognised it – it was where Doreen and her henchmen had taken me and where poor Andy had got his brains blown out. I looked across to where they shot him and the images of him came flooding back, lying there with blood pissing out his head and I remembered the smell of his brains and I nearly threw up. When I regained my composure I looked across at the dodgy looking bloke sitting behind the desk and he showed me to the scooters. I loaded them up and got away as quick as I could. I weren't stupid. I knew that something very dodgy was coming into the country via them scooters, but I done the old ostrich trick and buried my head. I weren't interested and, as long as they left me alone, I weren't bothered. In any case, after seeing what they done to Andy, just to show me they don't fuck about, I thought it was best I stayed that way.

CHAPTER 3

DEALING WITH DEATH

Yep three years had gone by since all the shit with Mike Warren and for once in my life I felt settled. When I was a kid I never really knew what I wanted; all I knew was that I didn't want to end up like my Dad in a dead end job, clocking in every day. The reality was that's exactly what I ended up doing and it scared the shit out of me. That's why I was a Mod – I felt like I was a cut above the rest 'cos I belonged to something and I had respect from my mates. We lived for the weekends, so it didn't matter about all the old bollocks I got at work during the week. Looking back, I think I expected and demanded too much from being a Mod. I should have took it for what it was – a laugh, a bit of fun, a bit of escapism. I was never happy at home as my Dad represented everything I didn't want from life and I despised him for it. My Mum didn't understand me; she always had more time for Sarah. I felt let down by family life, just like I felt let down by Mod after that crazy weekend in Brighton. Prison was fucking horrendous, but being part of Jack Warren's mob gave me a sense of security, a sense of belonging, similar to when I first discovered Mod. It was different though 'cos I never at any time felt let down; I was just fucking unlucky. Now I can sit back and smile because I didn't end up like my Dad and I am someone; I'm Jimmy, the crazy Mod who owns a night club. I get very little respect from

Roger, Vinny and all the other dodgy geezers I have to deal with occasionally, but I don't give a shit 'cos I get all the respect I need from the Mod and scooter scene. Call me immature, call me a prat, but I don't give a shit 'cos I have a great life, and this time I'm not looking at the Mod scene to fill a gap that's missing in my life as I'm blissfully happy at home with my gorgeous wife Tracy. The scene is what it should have been all along: a bit of fun that shouldn't be taken too serious.

I was doing so well with the club that Roger gave me his Saturday nights. He'd lost interest and set his sights on bigger things like hiring out leisure centres for his raves and all other kinds of shit with Ray. Vinny was never really that into the club, in fact, most Friday nights he didn't even turn up! Instead he'd work for Dave, driving hookers about. I don't know why he done it, but it certainly wasn't for the money… maybe he just preferred women's company.

It was the summer of '94 when I ended up having the Friday nights as well. At last I was back in full control of The Punch Bowl, which was great. We kept Thursday night as the sixties night and Friday and Saturday we had tribute bands on. I loved it. It was pure self-indulgence. I was well respected within the Mod scooter scene, not just because I ran one of the few clubs devoted to Mod, but I also owned the bike shop, which now Steven's involved, has become one of the biggest importers and restorers of scooters. For once in my life I felt totally secure and happy and I didn't think anything could go wrong. I was forty-seven and after everything I'd been through, I thought I could cope with anything life chucked at me. How wrong could I be?

It was a Thursday night and, as usual, everyone had a great night. The doorman had kicked the last punters out at midnight and Tracy was collecting up all the empties with Sandra, the bar maid.

Normally, Tracy gets a lift home with Sandra while I lock up before heading home at about one o'clock on my scooter. On this particular night Tracy stayed behind 'cos we had a water leak in the basement. There was water pissing everywhere so I called an emergency plumber out, but he couldn't get to us for at least an hour. I told Tracy to take the scooter home 'cos getting a taxi at that time would have been a nightmare. By the time the plumber had finished it was two o'clock and he gave me a lift home. We couldn't go the normal way 'cos the old bill had closed the road due to an accident. When we pulled up outside my house I knew something weren't right – there was no lights on and my scooter weren't on the drive. The kids were staying with their dad so I knew Tracy would have waited up for me and I had this horrible feeling in my stomach. I started to panic and begged the plumber to take me back to where the accident was. As we pulled up the police were reopening the road. I got out and ran up to one of the coppers.

"Oi mate, what 'appened 'ere"?

"It looks like a hit and run. Some poor cow on a scooter was knocked off – probably by a drunk".

"Fucking hell. It's my wife, Tracy".

"You'd better jump in. They've taken her to Lister".

"How is she? She's alright ain't she"?

"I don't know mate. I just had to reopen the road".

The copper radioed through to another copper who was at the hospital to let them know we were on our way. As soon as I walked through the hospital entrance I was approached by a doctor and a copper. Their faces said it all before their mouths even opened – my beautiful wife was dead. I was numb. I just sat in a chair with my head in my hands. I could hear voices, but nothing was registering. The doctor squeezed my arm gently to get my attention and told me I would need to identify Trace. The copper wanted to ask me some questions, but I wasn't ready – I wasn't ready for my wife to be dead. My head was buzzing with a million thoughts. I knew I couldn't go in there to identify her. I didn't want my last image of her to be of her lying dead in a hospital. I wanted to remember her looking stunning as ever in her blue dress, giving me a kiss and a cuddle, and looking back at me with that beautiful smile as she pulled away on my scooter. I rang Ken and he was at the hospital within fifteen minutes.

I've been through a lot in my life including tremendous feelings of dread and fear. When I looked back on my life, as I do quite often, I didn't think anything could be worse than serving three years in prison then, a week before my release date, getting another five years. Losing Tracy was a feeling I'd never experienced before and the loss just crushed me. I lost interest in everything: the club, the shop, the house, and even the kids, who moved back with their Dad. Life didn't seem worth living anymore and, if it weren't for Judy turning up one night, I would have done what I'd contemplated doing back in '65.

"Alright Jim? You gonna let me in"?

"Yeah, yeah. Come in. You're looking good".

"I wish I could say the same for you. You look like shit".

"I feel like shit. Do yer want a drink"?

"I'll have a cup of tea, thanks".

"Sure you don't want something a bit stronger"?

"No. I don't need it and neither do you. Look at the state of you! You need to snap out of it Jim. I know losing Tracy must be devastating, but your life don't have to end as well".

"Don't it? And why's that then"?

"Before Tracy died there were lots of things that made you happy. Tracy was a big part of it, but all those other things are still there".

"None of it seems right anymore. I can't just get pissed, go down the club and act like nothing's 'appended".

"You've got nothing to feel guilty for, Jim. I think that's exactly what you should do 'cos it's what Tracy would want. Do you think moping around, getting pissed on your own, looking like shit and feeling sorry for yourself is making her happy"?

"Well she ain't fucking 'ere is she so it don't matter".

"She is Jim. She'll always be with you and one day, when your time's up, you'll be together again in the spirit world. Then, when there's no-one living that can remember you, your spirits will be given a new life".

"You really believe all that old bollocks don't yer"?

"It's not bollocks Jim. Spirits are all around us, guiding us and helping us. You believe in karma don't you"?

"I have to say since 'aving that heavy-duty dope smoking session with you and your hippy mates when I got out the nick, I've seen a lot of horrible fuckers get their come-uppance".

"You do good things Jim then good things happen to you, just like if you do shitty things then you get it back. Spirits control that Jim. You're being watched and judged all the time. If it had been the other way round and you were killed you wouldn't want Tracy spending the rest of her life unhappy would you"?

"No I wouldn't. I loved her and I'd want her to be happy".

"Course you would and that's exactly what I'd want for you, so snap out of it and sort yourself out. Life's all about chapters Jim and Tracy has been a big chapter in your life, but you've got to move on".

Judy was right and when I listened to her talk I could totally see were she was coming from, but when I was in the house on my own at night all I could think about was Tracy. Everywhere I looked there was a constant reminder: the hairdryer on the side in the kitchen, the make-up left by the mirror in the dining room, her favourite dress hanging on the outside of the door to the wardrobe, all ready for the Friday night that never happened. For me to move on I had to remove these constant reminders of her physical presence, so I could accept her spiritual presence. People might think I was really losing the plot, but it helped me to talk to her.

It was a Saturday morning about six months after she'd died that I opened the curtains and the sun blinded me. There was kids playing with a football in the street, the miserable old git next door was cleaning his car, and the sexy blonde who lived opposite was getting out of a cab with her mate, laughing and giggling all the way to the front door as they swapped stories about what they'd been up to last night. I don't know if it was the sun or seeing how life carries on, but I finally had hope. This was it. I wasn't gonna give up. I decided to clear all Tracy's gear out then go to the bike shop, get another scooter and go for a ride. I started downstairs, boxing up all her books, videos, shoes and coats, before then moving on to the bathroom and clearing all her make-up and hair conditioners away. I was doing really well and I felt strong and positive, ready to tackle the bedroom. I walked in and said out loud, "right Trace, at last, I'm gonna have more room in the wardrobe". The wardrobe had been a constant battle between us 'cos there was never enough room, but Tracy always won and my clothes ended up in the cupboard on the landing. I opened the wardrobe door, black sack ready to fill. I should have just scooped the whole lot off the hangers in one go, but instead I took each blouse, each dress and each skirt out individually, every one bringing back a happy memory. I only got a quarter way through when the tears started to well up and I finally cracked, crumbling to the floor, when I got to her favourite dress. It was the one she wore on our wedding night; the one she saved for special occasions. She didn't have it cleaned too often because she didn't want to ruin it and there was a faint smell of her favourite perfume on it. I couldn't bring myself to screw it up and put it in a plastic sack destined for the charity shop, so I put it back. I had to get out, get away, but as I opened the front door ready to escape I was confronted by Vinny, standing there gormless as ever.

"Fuck me, Jim! That was quick. I didn't even ring the fucking bell".

"Out the way Vinny. I gotta get away from 'ere".

"'Ang on. Slow the fuck down. You ain't going nowhere until

you've stuck the kettle on and told me what's going on". Vinny grabbed my arm and pulled me in the house.

"Right Jim. Why are you in such a hurry to get out?"

"I woke up today and I was determined to move on, get on with my life and accept that Tracy was no longer a part of it. I started boxing all her stuff up, but when it came to her clothes I just couldn't bring myself to bag it all up for the charity shop. I guess I'm not ready yet."

"Get a fucking grip Jim. It's been six months! You drag this 'Woe is me. Poor Jim' act out any longer and we'll let yer get on with it."

"You're a heartless fucker, ain't yer? Well I don't need any of yer. You can all fuck off! Now I'm going out."

As I got up to leave Vinny stood up, pushed me back in the chair, leaned in towards me and said "right I'm going upstairs for a piss and you ain't going nowhere." While Vinny was upstairs I made another cup of tea. As I turned round to put the mugs on the table, Vinny was standing in the doorway with two black bin bags.

"There's all her clobber. Are you gonna bin 'em or am I?"

I couldn't believe it. There he was with her entire wardrobe stuffed into two bags and hanging out the top of one of them was Tracy's special dress.

"You bastard. That was her favourite dress".

"What, was it yours as well? What are yer – some sort of fucking tranny"?

"Fucking hell Vinny! Ain't you got any compassion at all"?

"Yeah course I 'av. That's why I'm round 'ere sorting out your missus' old fucking clothes and trying to sort you out too. In case you hadn't noticed, people are pissed off with yer moping about. Apart from Judy who else has bothered coming round"?

"I ain't seen anyone for a while".

"People don't need it Jim. We've all got fucking problems. You, me, Dave, Ron, Charlie – you ain't got the exclusive on fucking grief mate. I tell yer what would do you good: come and do a couple of nights driving for Dave, listen to some of the stories them girls have got to tell, then perhaps you won't feel so fucking sorry for yourself".

"Yeah I can imagine".

"When I first started driving them about I used to ask how they got into being hookers and some of the stories were horrendous".

"Abused as kids. that sort of thing"?

"Yeah a lot of the time, but some are junkies doing it for drugs and you've got young mums who can't work during the day because they've got no-one to "av the kids. There's girls who are too thick or lazy to get proper jobs and you've got party girls who just love a good time. They like their designer handbags and clothes and shagging geezers for money gives them that lifestyle. The way they figure it is why go out on a Friday night and shag someone for nothing when they can get paid for it"?

"Earn much do they"?

"They get a hundred quid an hour but a lot of them do extras. I've seen girls come out of a four hour booking with a couple of grand".

"Jesus what do they do for that"?

"You wouldn't believe what some of these sick fuckers want".

"Well what do they get for their hundred quid then"?

"Basic service, which is a shag or a blow job with a Johnny on. Anything else is extra".

"So what are the extras then"?

"Fucking 'ell Jim, use your imagination! You did 'av a sex life with Tracy didn't yer"?

"Course I fucking did. So if a geezer wanted to kiss them that costs more"?

"Yeah".

"Fucking "ell. The geezer who paid the two grand must have wanted a lot".

"He's a right dirty bastard. You wouldn't believe what he

wanted."

"Go on then, you built it up so you might as well tell us".

"Well, he sat at the table all done up in his best dinner jacket as if he was eating out at the Ritz, then the girl knelt on the table in front of him and shit on his plate. He ate it. The dirty bastard didn't even put any ketchup on it".

Vinny was pissing himself laughing as he was telling me, but I couldn't see the funny side – I just wanted to throw up.

"Fuck off. You're winding me up".

"Nah, honest mate. There's some sick fuckers out there; we've got geezers who drink piss and some just wanna be pissed on".

"Pissed on"?

"Yeah we've got this Catholic priest who shags the girls and then prays for forgiveness".

"At least he acknowledges he's done wrong".

"Yeah but while he's kneeling down in the shower cubicle praying he has the girl pissing all over him".

"Fucking Catholic priest as well, I suppose it's better than shagging the choir boys. Fucking hypocrites ain't they"?

"They're all as bad as each other mate. In fact, Pakis are our best customers".

"Why's that then"?

"Apparently they've got the smallest dicks and they've usually shot their load within about twenty seconds".

"You sound like you love it".

"I do mate. There's never a dull moment 'cos every night's different. Some of the girls are a right laugh. The other night I took two girls to a party job".

"What, like a house party"?

"Nah, a party job is a couple of coke heads wanting girls to get coked up with. They usually come in from two onwards. Anyway I took Justine and Amanda, a couple of English girls, to this big house out in the sticks, where these geezers had been on the gear all night. The bloke who owned the house said his missus weren't due back till ten the next day. Anyway the girls were due out at seven. I pulled up outside at seven on the dot and they came running out to the car, pissing themselves laughing. What had happened was they assumed 'cos it was a fucking big house that they must be loaded, so when they extended for the last two hours they didn't get the money up front. The one who didn't live there said he'd get it out the cash point at six. Course, he fucked off at six, left his mate passed out in the kitchen and didn't come back. The girls were mighty pissed off because they've got to pay the office out of their money, so they went to the stable, got this horse and put it in the geezer's kitchen. They locked the door and threw the key in the pond. Imagine explaining that one to the missus the next day"!

"Poor geezer".

"Fuck it mate. You wait till you've been doing the job a while you 'av little sympathy for the punters. They're not all arseholes though. Some of them are alright".

"Do you ever get any aggro"?

"Sometimes. The other night the office rung me and said 'quick! it's kicking off with Bianca'. I've went flying down Barnet High Street and there she was, threatening to cut this geezers throat".

"Fucking 'ell. What did he do"?

"He held her down and kissed her".

"You're joking".

"No, serious mate. Most of the girls don't do kissing".

"'Ang on a minute. They think nothing of sucking a geezer's cock, but they won't kiss 'em"?

"That's right".

"So 'ave you had to get heavy with any of them"?

"Not very often. I did have one geezer accuse me of trying to rape him".

"Rape him"?

"Yeah it was fucking funny. I took this French bird, Loretta, to a hotel job at Heathrow. She went in at twelve and the office rang at five to tell me to go up to the room as he's took the money back. I went up and the door was open, so I went in and there was this smarmy looking fucker sitting behind this desk. I asked him what the problem was and he said there weren't no problem, he just wasn't paying. I was like 'well, there is a fucking problem mate because I want five hundred quid. She came in at twelve and she's leaving at five'. The cocky fucker told me to call the old bill. I went over to get the money and he called the manager. Fucking bastard. When the manager came in I told him the situation and asked him to ring the police. Course, when I done that the geezer shits himself and says he'll pay, he just needed to go down to the cash machine in the lobby. I knew the fucker was gonna do a runner 'cos Loretta had already had the money and he'd snatched it back".

"What if the old bill turned up? Weren't you worried"?

"Nah, we ain't doing nothing illegal. They can't prove he paid for sex. Anyway, we all go down to get the money and the hotel manager makes me and Loretta wait in his office while he gets it. That gave us a chance to get our stories straight in case the coppers did turn up. I told her to say he slapped her and threw her on the bed as I walked in the room. About five minutes later the receptionist came flying in the office and said he punched the manager and legged it, so I went flying out the hotel and chased him across the car park and on to the lawn. I kicked his legs away and jumped on top of him, but bear in mind this was in front of a coach full of Japanese tourists that were all taking pictures, he started shouting 'he's trying to rape me!'. I'd had enough by this time so I stuck his head in a puddle – I wanted to drown the fucker. Finally the hotel manager said the police were on the way, so I picked him up and straight away he took a swing at me, so I strangled the fucker with his tie. I only eased off because the manager said he was going blue. The old bill turned up mob-handed, five of 'em! This geezer was a complete nutter; he wanted to press charges for assault, so I said 'Fine. So do we 'cos he hit Loretta'".

"So did you get your money"?

"Yeah. After a lot of fucking about".

Vinny told me more stories and it sounded a bit of a laugh.

"I might just do that. I'm not in the mood for the club and I can't sleep at night, so yeah… why not"?

"I've gotta pop down the office to cash up from last night. Do yer wanna lift"?

"No. You're alright. I'll pop down later. I'm gonna finish what I started here".

Vinny gave me the kick up the arse I needed. I'd got past the hurdle of Tracy's clothes, so I loaded all her stuff in the car to drop it off at the charity shop on the way to see Dave.

I don't see much of Dave. In fact, prior to Tracy's funeral, I'd probably seen him a dozen times in the last four years, if that. I like Dave and I still class him as my best mate, but he's trouble. I know he's mixed up with Roger and Ray so I've just kept my distance. I'm squeaky clean; the Old Bill, Roger, Ray, no-one's got anything on me. All the hassle with Mike Warren scared the shit out of me and since 1990 I've ploughed all my energy in to The Punch Bowl and surrounded myself with, I hate to say it, 'normal' people – blokes like Ron and Charlie. I've known them since the crazy days of the sixties and, although I liked 'em, I never made much effort over the years to really get to know 'em. I suppose the reason for that is the same reason I now 'ave all the time in the world for 'em – they're normal. They both got married young, had kids, kids grew up and they grew apart from their wives and ended up getting divorced.

That's the thing ain't it? You either grow together with your wife or you go in different directions. 'Aving kids is a big factor in all that. I can remember when I was inside, I'd done three years before my Mum and Dad bothered to visit me and even then it was only because I got moved down to the Scrubs and I was only a couple of stops away on the bus. Anyway, when they did visit me I remember thinking how much they'd changed and they'd said it was a lot different once me and Sarah had left home. I don't think they regretted having us or resented us or anything, but when I was lying in that cold, miserable cell it played on my mind and made me feel even more worthless. It's a feeling that stuck with me for a long time and I think that's the reason I didn't want any kids of my own with Tracy. She already had two kids when I moved in with her so I never really felt pushed out or nothing. I weren't stupid. I knew she loved 'em more than me and that didn't bother me. I never tried being a Dad to them, so I was always Jimmy, Mum's crazy boyfriend. Their Dad has always been a major part of their lives so I guess it was inevitable that after Tracy dying they would go and live with him. Especially when I started to hit the bottle hard. Vinny was right: I think people had had enough of me moping around. I hadn't seen Ron and Charlie much since Tracy's death. Before, we were doing a lot together: I'd even persuaded them to get scooters and come on rallies with me. It didn't actually take a lot of persuading 'cos I think they really got a taste for it again after our little adventure on the Isle of Wight.

I dropped all Tracy's stuff off at the charity shop and I headed off to see Dave. It was about a ten minute drive to Dave's and in that short time I started having second thoughts. At one point I actually stopped the car and said out loud "Jimmy, what the fuck are you doing"? I had a gut feeling that I was making a big mistake. I carried on driving, but by the time I'd pulled up outside the bike shop I'd talked myself out of it. Instead of going upstairs to Dave's office, I went in to the shop to see Ken and Steve. I walked in past row after row of shiny new and restored scooters. Ken was behind the counter and Steve was round the back putting the finishing touches to another project he'd been working on. Ken looked up and shouted out to Steve. "Steve, stop what you're doing! Look what the cat's dragged in – it's Jim". Steve appeared from the back of the shop and, although he was putting nuts and bolts together, he looked immaculate: not a hair out of place and not a mark on his crisp clean Fred Perry shirt.

"Alright Jim? How you doing mate"?

"I'm alright. I'm getting there. I thought I'd come down and see yer, seeing neither one of yer 'ave bothered popping in to see me".

"Fuck off, Jim. We ain't been round 'cos you didn't want anyone round. You made that blatantly clear when we came round back in November".

"Yeah, you're right. I'm not 'aving a go".

"You ain't the only one suffering mate. I've lost my sister".

"And I lost my favourite aunt. We all loved her, Jim and we all miss her, but life goes on".

"Yeah, you're right. That's why I'm 'ere; the sun's out, the season's starting and I want another scooter".

"Dad, stick the kettle on and I'll show Jim what we've got". Steve's face lit up as he showed me to a line of restored Lambrettas he'd done up.

"What do yer fancy? We've got a nice SX, totally original, there's an LI, a TV or, if you fancy a change, a selection of GPs".

"Why don't you just 'ave a new Vespa? They're much better all round". Ken butted in.

"Fucking Vespa? Your old man still don't know fuck all about scooters does he"?

"Nah, bless him – he's trying".

"I tell yer what. I'll 'ave the SX".

"I'll fill it up and get it ready for yer".

I'd tried to hide my amazement at the difference I could see in the shop, but I couldn't fake it no more.

"I can't believe how you've turned this place around Ken".

"I couldn't have done it without Steve. We work well together even if he works like a fucking poof. Look at him! There ain't a mark on him and he even wears rubber gloves so he don't get oil on his fingers".

"Nothing wrong with personal pride, Ken".

Steve weren't taking it from Ken. "That's what I keep telling him. I don't wanna go out stinking of that shit he puts on his hands to get the oil off", He paused for a bit, "Now you're back on the road, do yer fancy coming for a ride on Sunday? The lads will be glad to see yer. They've all been asking about yer".

"Yeah, sure. Where you off to"?

"Nowhere special. Probably brekky at the Ace Café".

"Sounds good. Where we meeting – usual place"?

"Nah, we meet at the football ground. Be there for ten fuelled up".

"Look forward to it".

We pushed the scooter out the shop and tried starting it, but it was a tricky fucker. It wouldn't start, so I pushed it up and down the road trying to bump it. It was totally fucked, so I pushed it back to the shop where Dave was stood, laughing his bollocks off.

"Look at the state of you. You look like you're gonna have a fucking heart attack. Stop fucking around with it and come up. I've been waiting for yer".

CHAPTER 4

DAVE, JIMMY, and the RUSSIAN HOOKER

"He's your typical sex, drugs, and rock 'n'roll sort of geezer". That's how Jim described me and he's spot on: I love fast women, cars, boats, life, and drugs. I'm always looking for the next high; the next buzz, so what makes me me and Jim Jim? It all stems from our childhood and how we're brought up I suppose. Jim always struggled to be someone because his Dad was a useless cunt and, quite rightly, Jim didn't want to end up like him. Jim struggled whereas for me it came easily. Jim hated his Dad and what he represented, but I fucking loved my Dad.

He was a singer in a rock 'n' roll band and my Mum was a backing singer. I never knew my Mum 'cos she ran off with the drummer when I was just two years old. From what my Dad told me she was a bit of a slapper. Up to the age of ten I was passed around from one aunt to another and when they had had enough of me I'd stay with my Gran. At ten I was becoming a right little fucker and no-one wanted me, so my Dad had to stop touring and bring me up.

This was a serious hassle for my Dad because he was your original party animal. He was out a lot and he always seemed to bring a different bird home. I used to listen to them shagging away in the bedroom. Once I came down in the night to get a drink and he was in the living room having a threesome. I shouldn't really have watched I suppose, but it fascinated me.

When I was thirteen my Dad sat me down for a chat about women 'cos he couldn't understand why I didn't have a girlfriend. Before he started I told him not to bother as I knew all about shagging through what I'd seen and heard him getting up to over the last three years. I grew up way too quickly: at thirteen I was drinking, smoking, skipping school and I was even working with my uncle Bob at the weekends cleaning the cars at his garage. The only thing I weren't doing was shagging, much to my Dad's disappointment. A few days before my fourteenth birthday my Dad announced that he'd got to go away for a week. Initially I was well pissed off, thinking that I would have to go and stay with one of my boring aunts, but when Dad said that one of his girlfriend's mates had agreed to stay with me, I couldn't wait. Her name was Suzy and when she walked in I couldn't believe it – it was only one of the birds I'd seen my Dad have a threesome with. She was about five foot six, had brown hair and eyes, and was a bit chubby, but she had the biggest tits I'd ever seen. I weren't sure how old she was, probably mid to late twenties though. The one thing I did know was that she was one fucking horny bird. She moved in on the Monday and I couldn't wait for her to go to work so I could have a pervy rummage through her stuff. She had beautiful silk and lace knickers, stockings, suspenders, the lot. She was moving out on Saturday so there were five pairs of knickers. When she left for work on Tuesday I had a look to see what pair of knickers weren't there. I was staying in a house on my own with a horny bird and now I knew that when she walked in later, under that tight black skirt, she's got them little skimpy white knickers on. I didn't bother going to school; all I could think of the whole day was Suzy and what I'd like to do with her. By three o'clock I was beginning to get worried. What if it was true and you really did go blind if you played with your cock too much? Suzy got in at about half five and, to my disappointment, she went straight upstairs to have a bath. I followed her up the stairs and her arse wiggled at my eye level. I was in heaven. When she got to the top, she walked in the bathroom, turned to look back at me and gave a dirty smile before locking the door. I can remember feeling robbed at the time. I wanted to sit opposite her eating my dinner knowing what knickers she had on, but my Dad always taught me to turn a negative situation into a positive one and the positive was that our bathroom door had a small glass panel above it. The only thing we had upstairs for me to stand on was a small bedside table. It weren't very big, but it had to do because if I brought a chair upstairs and she got out the bath too soon I wouldn't have been able to get it down quick enough. I put the table close to the door and climbed up to look through the window. There she was, lying there reading a book. The bath was in the perfect position for me to look without her noticing me. I couldn't see her tits very well because her arms were in the way, but I had a great view of her pussy. She took fucking ages reading the book and, although this was the first time I'd actually seen a woman's pussy, I was starting to get bored and my legs were aching because of the way I was precariously balancing on the table. Just as I was about to give up and climb down she put the book down and started rubbing soap in to those beautiful huge tits, which immediately made my cock start to get hard again. She worked her way down her belly and by the time she'd got to her pussy there was no soap on her hands, but she was still rubbing her pussy. I thought to myself that perhaps women don't use soap on their pussies before I realised by the way she was softly moaning that she weren't washing it; she was playing with herself. It was fucking amazing – like watching a live porn film! She started moaning a bit louder, then her stomach tensed up, her toes pointed out straight, her hands moved faster and all of a sudden the fucking table collapsed.

I fell and hit my head on the door handle and ended up lying on the floor, blood pissing out my head with my cock in my hand. She shouted

"What the fuck's going on"?

I panicked and the first thing I could think of was, "Fucking dog! I tripped over him and hit my head on the door". I heard her get out the bath pretty sharpish and I can remember thinking "shit! What do I do first?" I didn't have enough time to put my cock away, pick the broken table up, and drag the dog upstairs. As the bathroom door opened I was standing there holding the broken table.

"Dave what are you doing"?

"I was taking this table into the other room and the dog ran out in front of me and I tripped up."

She weren't stupid she knew exactly what I'd been doing and the rest of the week she constantly teased me. The week went too quickly until Friday, she'd got dressed for work and was in the kitchen doing herself a packed lunch. She had a tight black skirt on with stockings and she knew I was watching her. She pretended to have an itch at the top of her leg and, as she put her hand up her skirt, I could see her stocking top. God, she was horny.

All week she'd kept me in fantasies and I was gutted she was going the next day. I had been hoping that I might get the chance to shag her, but I was a fourteen year old virgin and she was a stunning woman. Why would she be interested in me? She got ready to go out on that Friday night and she looked gorgeous; she had a bright red dress on, and underneath it I knew she had black bra, knickers and stockings. She went out and I stayed in watching TV. All night I was thinking some lucky bastard is gonna end up shagging her. At about midnight there was a knock on the door and, as I opened it, Suzy fell in. She was well pissed. She staggered to the living room and flopped back on the settee, asking me to get her a drink of water. As I gave her the glass she said,

"So Dave, why hasn't a good looking boy like you got a girlfriend"?

I said I did, but she didn't believe me. She just giggled then patted the settee saying,

"Come and sit next to me".

I sat next to her and she turned her head to me and said,

"Did you enjoy watching me in the bath"?

There was no point denying it. She knew. I never felt embarrassed because she was pissed, so I said,

"Yeah, I did".

"What's the best bit about me you like"?

"You've got great tits". She smiled.

"Would you like to touch them"?

She didn't have to ask twice! I was thinking all my Christmases had come at once. I was sitting on her right, so I leaned over and with my right hand I began squeezing her left tit. Even though I was touching it through her dress and bra, I could feel her huge nipple stiffening up. She pulled my face to hers and started kissing me. The smell of gin on her breath didn't put me off and my flies were at bursting point as my cock hardened up. As she was flicking her tongue in and out of my mouth, I was frantically battling with the buttons on the front of her dress. I managed to undo them down to the black belt around her waist. I had my left arm behind her neck and I pulled her forward so I could undo her bra. I was fucking around for ages trying to unclip it and, instead of her helping me, she just pulled the front of her bra down to expose those beautiful tits. I instantly stopped kissing her and started sucking on her huge nipples, while my hands started to explore up her dress. I slipped my right hand up the inside of her leg until I got to the top of her stockings. As my fingers slipped over her stocking top to her bare leg, she opened her legs and I started rubbing her pussy through her silky knickers. She leaned over me and started to undo my flies, pulling my trousers and pants down and rubbing my cock. The whole time she was gradually kissing her way down my chest. I remember thinking "My God, she's gonna suck my cock!" The mere thought of it was too much and I shot my load. She stopped what she was doing, giggled and said "better luck next time". I quickly got up, went to the toilet to sort myself out and when I came back in she'd taken herself off to bed. I was gutted. It was the first real chance to lose my virginity and I blew it. I sat there for about an hour feeling sorry for myself before deciding to go to bed. As I walked past her bedroom though, I couldn't resist one last chance to have a look. The door was open, so I stepped in to find her lying face down on the bed, still fully clothed. I asked her if she was alright, but she was out of it. Looking back now, I know it was wrong on so many levels, but I couldn't resist having a little fiddle. I mean, when would I get a chance like that again? I lifted her dress over her hips and slid her knickers off. She didn't move so I gently parted her legs and started to touch her pussy. As I was slipping my fingers in and out, she started to moan and groan, and she rolled over, grabbed me and started kissing me. That night I lost my virginity. It was amazing. I woke up in the morning and looked into her bedroom, but she wasn't there, so I rushed down stairs thinking she'd be doing breakfast. The only thing in the kitchen was a note on the table saying, "We had some fun, but please don't say anything and it will never happen again." I was gutted 'cos I thought she really liked me and would want to do it again, but the truth was, to her, it was just a bit of drunken fun. To me it meant the world, but to Suzy it meant nothing. With a childhood like that and losing my virginity in such a spectacular way, it's no wonder I turned out like I did.

I love sex; it's the most natural thing in the world. I don't associate sex with love. I know when you love someone you have sex with them, but what I mean is the two don't have to go together: some of the best sex I've had has been on one night stands. I think people make too much of a big deal about sex. Virtually every day you can read in the paper about some scandal with politicians or celebrities or vicar or priest, murders, messy divorce, broken families, devastated kids, bribery, blackmail, governments have fallen blah blah blah… and what's at the bottom of it all? Sex; the most natural thing in the world. So what makes me think my flippant view towards sex is right and the vast majority of the human race has got it wrong? Well, a few years back when AIDS hit the news, it didn't bother me because, like everyone else, I thought it only affected queers, but when it emerged that anyone who was promiscuous could get it I panicked. Me and Bunny both got checked out and were given a clean bill of health. It shit the life out of Bunny and she wanted us to knock it on the head a bit and not shag around so much. She done really well, but I just couldn't stop; sex was like a drug to me. It was starting to cause a few rows between us, she reckoned I had a real problem. She was right. I was addicted to sex. She booked me in for some counselling sessions and, although I weren't too keen, I gave it a go for her.

The counsellor was a nice enough bloke and what he said made a lot of sense. He reckoned that because I never had my Mum around as a kid, I was deprived of love, and losing my virginity in the way I did at such a young age has affected the way I view sex and women. I could see all that. I mean most kids lose their virginity in the normal way – they fancy someone at school, get all giggly and get their mate to ask them out for them. They have their first kiss, then they progress to a bit of touching up. They start to fall in love and eventually they end up shagging. This is the right way because they then associate sex with love. I get all that, but the counsellor weren't offering me a cure; he was just telling me why I was a dirty bastard.

I did want to change because I really loved Bunny, so I tried to cure myself. When me and Bunny were hiding away from the Jamaicans we had plenty of time on our hands, so I started reading different books on sex and religion. I figured that if I had such a problem with sex then I would have to get to the bottom of why it was the big 'I AM'. What I read was fascinating. I can quote what Saint Paul said about sex along with various other prominent religious figures throughout history, but I won't bore you. The bottom line is, sex is such a big deal because of the fucking church. It's ironic that throughout history millions of people have been killed and countless lives ruined in the name of religion and a misguided belief in God or fucking Allah. The one thing the churches should embrace is sex. It creates life, it makes people happy, it's pleasure for young and old, rich or poor, but the church don't like it. They see it as a necessary evil for the human race to continue. They invented marriage because their view is if you must have sex then you should have one partner. They come up with all these bullshit vows that you shouldn't break and they won't allow priests and nuns to have sex. I bet most Catholics can tell you a story about a wicked nun. Why? They're sexually frustrated and miserable! Practically every day you read about some fucking poof of a priest fucking around with choir boys. It's not right to take away a man or woman's natural urges for sex.

I set out to cure myself because I thought I had an over the top appetite for sex, but being cooped up in that flat for so long I came to the conclusion that it weren't me with the problem – it was every other fucker. So, rather than tone my interest in sex down, I went the other way and established the biggest escort agency in the country. I've always dabbled in prostitution: when we had our place in Kent I had five very nice girls, I used to set up for very wealthy clients. I weren't a pimp though 'cos I never took a penny of what they earned. I made my money from the drugs and the membership they paid the club. When we torched the house for the insurance, the plan was to pay off the Jamaicans and have enough money to go abroad to somewhere like Spain. We lost everything in the house, but like my Dad always advised, we turned a negative into a positive. I figured if the rich were paying hookers then, if you made the price cheap enough, your average bloke in the street would. You've always had your street walkers. They're usually heroin addicts that are well rough and looked after by scumbag pimps. There's never any shortage of dirty old gits who just want a quick shag down an alley or in the back of their car. I set out to bridge that gap between the low and the high class hookers. I kept in contact with a few of the girls and they helped me set up my agency 'A Touch of Class Escorts'. It took a while to convince them to go out for fifty quid an hour because they were used to being booked for five hundred for the night. It does sound a lot, but they would only do one or two nights a week. The deal was that we charged the punter one hundred quid an hour, the girl got fifty, the driver twenty, and the agency thirty. Within six months I was raking it in. I had twenty girls on each night and I was clearing about ten grand a week.

When Vinny said Jim wanted to do a bit of driving, I weren't too sure it was a good idea because Jim's a bit gullible at the best of times and since Tracy died he's an emotional wreck. I stood watching him trying to start that scooter and I thought, "Fuck it. I'll give him a chance."

"You coming up or not"?

"Yeah. Stick the kettle on".

"So Jim, you wanna do a bit of driving then"?

"I ain't sure to be honest. how does it work and what's it all about"?

"It's simple, mate. I give you a call at about 6.30 and tell you who you're picking up and where from, you pick them up at 7.30, but you don't knock on the door".

"Why not"?

"Because some of them have got husbands and boyfriends

that ain't got a clue what they're doing".

"You're joking. No way".

"Yeah, straight up. So give the office a call when you're outside".

"So when they're in the car, what do I do, come 'ere"?

"Yeah, if she ain't booked straight away bring her here".

"Then what"

"You wait until she's booked. We've got a pool table, dartboard, TV, or you can wait in your motor and have a kip. When she's booked I'll send her down. When you take her to the address you wait outside until she goes in, then park round the corner and ring to tell us she's in. Then you just wait until she comes out".

"So how much do I get"?

"Right, when she gets back in the car she's got to give you fifty quid for every hour she's in there; you keep twenty and the office gets thirty. You cash in when you've got five hundred. Is that all clear? You look a bit puzzled. Is there a problem mate"?

"Yeah; I don't know if I can do it. It don't seem right".

"And why's that then Jim"?

"Well… making money out of what these poor cows do".

"Poor cows! Listen mate, they're on about fifteen hundred a week. Bank managers and company directors don't get that".

"It's alright for you 'cos you've never really had much respect for women. You shag 'em and move on to the next, but these girls that are making you money are all someone's daughter".

"Listen mate, I've got plenty of respect for women, especially the girls doing this job 'cos it takes a fucking lot of guts to do what they do. As for them being someone's daughter, they're daughters of parents that have fucked their heads up. Not all of them mind, but a good per cent have had shit lives. These girls ain't prim and proper little girls fresh out of Swiss finishing schools; they're damaged goods and they're the most manipulative girls you'll ever meet. Don't start feeling sorry for them. No-one's got a gun to their head forcing them to be hookers. The ones you should feel sorry for are the mug punters that they suck in and spit out once the money runs out".

I started driving for Dave and I have to say Vinny was right: it did do me good. When Tracy died the only way I could cope with the emptiness I felt inside was to drink. Tracy was such a massive part of my life and I couldn't see how I could carry on without her. There was no shortage of well-intentioned people telling me how life goes on and that I would get over her in time. They meant well, but I didn't want to get over her. She was in my thoughts every minute of the day.

I would start the night drinking, fully intending to not wake up the next day. When I was sober I was depressed, but as soon as I started drinking I'd cast my mind back to all the good times. I'd sit there laughing to myself before I remembered the times that weren't so nice, like when I was in prison or how lost and let down I felt with life when I was just eighteen. It's when I got to that point that I usually snapped out of it because I was on the verge of ending it all. If you had said to me a week before Tracy died, "do you regret not topping yourself back in sixty-five?" I would have said, "don't be fucking stupid. Look at the life I've had and still got." Judy was right – life is chapters. I'm not sure what the future holds. I'm still confused and mixed up half the time, but compared to some of the stories I hear from the girls I've met driving for Dave, my life's a bed of fucking roses.

When I first started driving the girls, I asked a lot of question and, some of the girls chatted all night, but some just told me to mind my own fucking business. Like Dave and Vinny said; girls do the job for all different reasons, but the vast majority did have fucked up childhoods. I got to the point where I didn't ask too many questions. If they wanted to talk then I talked. I like to think I gave some good advice and helped a few of them. Some of the disgusting stories Vinny had told me were hard to believe. I thought I knew it all and was pretty open-minded, but some of the things these punters wanted was fucking bizarre, to say the least.

Dave was right about feeling sorry for the punters. You wouldn't believe how gullible and fucking stupid some of them are. They actually believe that when they see the same girl on a regular basis that they will fall in love with them. The punters are just as varied as the girls though, and I hear some very sad stories like this young bloke called Tony. Tony was twenty-eight. He played football on a Sunday, squash during the week and, like most young blokes, he went out on the pull Friday and Saturday night. He had a good job and a bright future until he was involved in a horrific car crash, which left him minus a leg and with a badly disfigured face. His days of pubbing and clubbing were over. The only beautiful girls he was ever going to make love to were the ones he paid each week with his compensation money. When the girls went in there for the first time they were shocked and horrified and some walked out. The ones that stayed were treated like princesses and Tony showed them photos of what he looked like before the accident, which helped when eventually he made love to them. The girls were his one pleasure in life and when his money ran out he planned to end it all.

I tried not to get too close to the girls 'cos I was still an emotional wreck and I was never sure whether the girls were taking the piss out of me. There was one girl called Sally who was about thirty. She was nice looking, but no stunner and she weren't very busy. Some nights all she earned was enough money to pay for her fags and the babysitter, so I'd help her out sometimes. She used to talk about her daughter all the time and you could tell she loved her to bits. One night I was talking to one of the drivers and I mentioned to him about Sally and he reckoned she was a heroin addict and the money I gave her just got her the next fix. He reckoned she didn't even have a daughter. I picked her up the next night and confronted her with what I'd heard and she didn't deny it. She told me all about her life and how she'd been abused by her Step-dad and Step-brother and how her Mum hadn't believed her. She left home when she was sixteen and lived with her aunt. She got in a lot of trouble and ended up getting into drugs. She had her daughter when she was twenty and she stayed off the drugs, but when her boyfriend left her she went off the rails again and Social Services put her daughter in care. She loved her daughter, but she couldn't get off the heroin. I don't know to what extent she was abused as a kid, but she just couldn't get over it and the heroin helped. I took her out on a Friday night and she saw a particularly nasty punter. It was eight o'clock Saturday morning when she came out and she was in a right state. She said she'd had enough and she was going to visit her aunt in Dorset so she asked me to drop her at the train station. She never got on the train. She jumped in front of it instead. I was gutted. I should have realised what she was gonna do. I felt guilty and decided I'd had enough of hearing sad stories, so I went down the office to tell Dave.

"I can't do it no more. Vinny was right; it's certainly put my life into perspective".

"You shouldn't get so involved, Jim. You're their driver not a fucking counsellor. I'll tell yer what – give it one last chance. There's this new Russian girl I want you to pick up".

"Great. What am I gonna 'ave in common with a fucking Russian"?

"Probably fuck all, but you're driving her around, not taking her on a fucking date. You don't need to know the ins and outs of her poxy little life, so keep it simple for fuck's sake".

"Yeah, well, we've still gotta talk ain't we"?

"She'll talk alright. In fact, she talks too much 'cos she's not been here long so she asks a lot of questions. At one point I thought she might be some sort of undercover cop".

"So why don't yer get rid of her? From what you say, there's no shortage of girls".

"'Cos she's fucking good. The punters love her! Some of the things I was hearing back... there's no way she's a copper. She only works Thursday, Friday and Saturday and she's always booked before she leaves the house".

"Fine, but Dave, I was talking to one of the girls and she reckons some of the drivers are dealing".

"Yeah. Some of the drivers do a bit of dealing".

"Fucking drugs. When are you gonna learn"?

"I ain't dealing. I just put Ray and Roger onto those who are. The only drugs I buy are for mine and Bunny's personal use".

"Dave, I don't wanna know what you're up to with them; all I wanna know is it ain't gonna involve me. Is it"?

"Course it ain't".

"Good. Give us this bird's address then and I'll get out of here. I need to get home and get ready".

"Her name's Nadia and you need to pick her up at 7.30. She's booked at Gatwick".

"Gatwick? That's fucking miles away"!

"Don't worry. It's one of her regulars and she'll be in there all night, so I'll see you tomorrow to cash up".

Dave was right. I'm not gonna get to know the girls too well. I was a bit worried when Dave said some of the drivers are dealing, but he's right: it ain't got fuck all to do with me. Dave will never learn. It was drugs that fucked him up last time.

I picked Nadia up at 7.30 and I couldn't believe how stunning she was. She had long blonde hair, big blue eyes, and her figure was amazing. She was like a model.

"Hello. What's your name? I've not seen you before".

"I'm Jimmy. No, I haven't been here long".

"I don't normally get picked up by new drivers – you're very lucky".

"Lucky? Why's that then"?

"Because I'm the busiest girl and Dave always lets one of the better drivers drive me".

"Well, me and Dave are mates. We go way back".

"You must be Jimmy from the club".

"How did you know that"?

"I've heard one of the other drivers talk about you".

"That must be Vinny".

"Yes I think it was".

"Your English is really good".

"Thank you. I've spent a lot of time here. Why are you driving me and not at your club"?

"It's a long story".

"Tell me. It will take one hour and thirty minutes before we are there".

"I'm just not in the mood for the club since my wife died".

"How did she die"?

"She was killed by a hit and run driver, probably some piss head, and the old bill never got him".

"You said it's a long story, but that was a very short story. Tell me about you and Dave instead. Do you deal drugs with him"?

"No I fucking don't. I have nothing to do with drugs".

"But you went to prison for a long time because you were a drug dealer"?

"Fucking hell! Dave was right".

"About what"?

"You. He said you ask a lot of questions".

I got to know Nadia really well and became her permanent driver. she asked a lot of questions and I really felt I could open up to her. I told her my whole life story and how all I ever wanted in life was a good time, but somehow I always managed to fuck up and get in the shit.

I was really enjoying the driving and getting on well with Nadia. In fact, too well. I was starting to have feelings for her and when she went with the clients I was starting to get jealous. Dave warned me when I started that they were the most manipulative girls you'd ever meet, so when I told him how I felt about her he just laughed.

"Fuck off Jim. Not again. When are you gonna learn? They're hookers, mate. They fuck blokes for money. This is an escort agency, not a fucking dating agency. I gave you a Russian to pick up because I didn't want to see you get in a state again like you did with Sally. I'll tell yer what – you can take one of the new Polish birds out. They talk fuck all English".

"No, don't do that. I'll be alright".

"I hope so Jim, because trust me, all Nadia is interested in is what she can get out of yer. I bet you've told her about the club and everything, ain't you"?

"I didn't have to. She already knew 'cos Vinny told her".

"What do yer mean Vinny told her? He's never met her".

So how did she know so much? It bothered me, so I went to see Vinny.

"Alright Jim? Come in mate. What can I do for yer"?

"I ain't seen yer about for a while and Dave said you ain't been driving. I just wondered what you're up to"?

"I've been driving, just not for Dave that's all. I'm thinking of starting my own agency up".

"That'll piss Dave off".

"I don't give a fuck. I tell yer what – the way Dave's going, he ain't gonna 'ave an agency much longer. He's more into fucking around with drugs with Roger".

"Yeah, that's what I thought, but I asked him about it and he swears he's not. He just puts Ray and Roger on to the drivers who're dealing. It did bother me".

"It fucking should do".

"When you was driving for Dave did you ever drive a Russian bird around called Nadia"?

"No, mate. There was a Russian bird there called Nadine who I drove a couple of times, but I didn't like her 'cos she asked too many questions".

"Yeah, this Nadia does".

"Jim, I don't mean to rush you off mate, but I'm meeting my sister at one".

"Yeah, no problem".

"Jim, watch yourself mate. Something's going on. I don't know what, but keep your head down. I'm off now to see Doreen".

CHAPTER 5

DOREEN, RAY, VINNY

I've got three sisters: Doreen's the eldest, then there's Stephanie, and the youngest is Karen. My Mum died having me, so Doreen brought me up and we never saw much of my Dad, Mike. He was always up to something or he was at his villa in Spain. Doreen was the closest to him. She looked more like him and she had more of his personality traits; she was alright with me, but I've seen her flip at the slightest thing and batter Stephanie and Karen. She always wanted to play a bigger part in Mike's firm, but he always kept her at a safe distance. She was definitely his favourite and when he started to get me involved with the firm she took it quite bad and didn't want much to do with me. Even when I got out the nick she kept her distance, but the final straw was when I helped Jimmy, Dave, Rudy and Roger fuck Mike over. So you can imagine that when I got a call from her saying she wanted to meet up I was well surprised.

I was meeting her in London at her apartment which overlooked the Thames. I didn't have a clue what she'd been up to since Mike's death, but whatever it was she must have been doing alright because these places were worth millions. I walked in to find a very stark and cold looking place. The walls were all white and there weren't much furniture; just a bright red leather armchair and two sofas. The paintings on the wall were just like splashes of bright red, like pictures of anger, and on the side by the phone was a picture of Mike. As I walked towards her there was no show of affection or a welcoming smile.

"It's been a long time Vinny. Sit down. What can I get you"?

"I'll have a beer".

She went to the fridge and got me a can, then poured herself what looked like a whisky from a very expensive looking crystal decanter. She sat opposite me and sipped her drink, just staring at me. I stared back for what seemed like ages she made me feel uneasy, scared even, so out of nervousness I said,

"So what's this? A fucking competition to see who's gonna blink first"? She smiled, took another sip of her drink and said,

"Competition? If it was I'd win every time; you're no competition for me 'cos we're in different leagues, Vinny".

"So what's this all about then? Why, after all this time, do you wanna see me"?

"Sit back Vinny, relax. We've got a lot of catching up to do". She put her drink on the glass coffee table that sat between us, put her jacket over the back of the sofa, kicked her shoes off, and sat back and smiled as she said,

"So what have you been up to since they killed Dad"?

"No-one killed Mike. He had a heart attack and you know it".

"Mike? He was your Dad"!

"Not to me he weren't. He was always Mike the gangster".

"No, you was never close, was you? Strange really, you being the only son and all that. I don't think he ever got over Mum dying while having you... So Vinny, what have you been getting up to"?

"I'll ask you again: why? Why do you wanna know? What possible use can I be to you? You're obviously doing alright 'cos this place alone must be worth millions".

"Do you like it"?

"I love it".

"I want to know because you're the only family I've got left and I think we can work well together".

"What about Karen and Stephanie? They're still about".

"Stephs' moving to Australia at the end of the year and Karen's moved down to the West Country with that useless prick of a husband".

"So how can we work well together"?

She looked agitated as she squeezed her glass so tight I thought it would shatter. The look on her face was a look I'd seen so many times on Mike's face, just before he'd fly into a fit of rage. I could feel myself tensing up, getting ready for her to blow a gasket, but instead she got up and poured herself another drink. She sat back down then said through clenched teeth,

"I'm not sure if we can. Perhaps you should just go back to your shitty go nowhere, do nothing, mundane life".

For a split second I nearly put my drink down, got up and walked out, but I took a moment to take on board what she said and when she put it like that I thought she was right. All of a sudden curiosity got the better of me and I thought I'd answer her original question to see if I could get another chance.

"So you wanna know what I've been up to since Mike died? Well I'll tell yer – Me, Jimmy and Roger became equal partners in The Punch Bowl".

"How did that come about? Dad owned that".

"No, he didn't. The Punch Bowl was always Jimmy's and he sold half of it to Roger. Well, he thought he did, but he didn't realise at the time what Roger was in to and he didn't know nothing about Mike".

"So how did you get a share of it then"?

"Mike promised me The Punch Bowl if I helped Jimmy bring his drugs back from the Isle of Wight. When Mike died and the firm was split up, it turned out that The Punch Bowl was always in Roger's name and he wanted to give Jim his half back. The two of them cut me in because if it weren't for me they couldn't have set Mike up. To start with running the club was a laugh 'cos there was always plenty of crumpet and the money was good. Jim run Thursday night, I had Friday, and Roger Saturday".

"So why did you end up driving hookers about"?

"Boredom. I was only working Friday night the rest of the week I was sitting in with a takeaway watching a load of shit on TV".

"Didn't you wanna go out with your mates"?

"You know me. I never had many mates".

"Many? You never had any, just like now".

"I've got mates! Not many, but there's Jimmy, Dave, Ken, Roger, Ron and Charlie".

"And that's it. No wonder you don't wanna do anything with them. Let's start with Ron and Charlie: a couple of slap dash builders who get their jollies riding round on scooters at the weekend with that useless git Jimmy".

"Jimmy's alright. He ain't useless".

"Yeah you're right. The other two are, but Jimmy's not as daft as you think. He just comes across like that. You don't manage to stash nearly two million quid in an offshore bank account through being daft do you"?

"'As he bollocks. The club's not doing that well and he sure as hell ain't making a fortune selling fucking bikes".

She smiled, put her drink down and walked across the room to a cabinet and shuffled through some paperwork. She took some documents out, walked back over to drop them on the table in front of me, saying,

"You really haven't got a clue have you"?

I looked through the document, which was a bank statement in a foreign language. Fuck knows what it said, but the things that were clear were the names at the top: Dave, Roger and Jimmy, and the amounts paid in, with a balance total of just under eight million.

"What the fuck is this"?

"A statement for an account that Alex - Dad's old accountant, set up for your so--called mates".

"I know it's a fucking statement, but how the fuck 'ave they managed to stash that amount of cash"?

"You really haven't got a clue, have you? They used you to help bring Dad down. Even your uncle Jack. His name's not on that statement because he's far too clever to be roped in with them, but he's laundered his money through his business empire".

"The only way they can make that kind of money is through drugs and there's no way Jimmy or Jack would get involved in that shit".

"You reckon, do you? Well, let me get you another beer and I'll explain".

She took the statements and my glass off the table and went to pour us both another drink. My head was throbbing with the million thoughts going through it. I started casting my mind back four years to when we went to the Isle of Wight, but I was confused. I couldn't work it out. In the short time it took her to put them documents back and pour the drinks, I was trying to make sense of it and think of a way they could have fucked me over. I couldn't see it, but there it was in black and white on that statement. She gave me my drink, then sat back on the sofa sipped her drink and began her explanation.

"Right, where shall I start? I won't go too far back because we'll be here all night, so let's take it back to your little adventure on the Isle of Wight. You were all going over there to bring back between ten and thirty million quid's worth of cocaine. Let's say it was twenty million's worth, for argument's sake. Why do you think that dumb coon Rudy took the bulk of it in a fucking great van while you lot brought a little bit back on scooters"?

"'Cos we didn't need a lot. All we needed was enough…"

Before I could say "enough to set Mike up" she snarled:

"Enough to set Dad up"?

"Yeah that's right".

"So if five million's worth was enough to set Dad up, how much do you think was enough for the Darkies to go down for"?

"The same I suppose".

"That's right and that's how much the Old Bill recovered, so where do you think the other ten million quid's worth went"?

"Fucking Rudy, no wonder he fucked off to the Caribbean".

"No, no, no, Rudy had his cut alright and he done really well, but the dumb shit didn't have the brains or the contacts to shift that amount of gear. No, that was down to Dave, Roger and your uncle Jack. By the time they'd paid that bent copper Charles off and you and the other clowns your poxy fifty grand, they were laughing".

"Nah, bollocks. Jack hated drugs and Jimmy wouldn't have had none of it. He was shit scared about going back inside".

"Jimmy didn't know nothing about it. They kept him well out of the picture and it was only when the dust settled and Jimmy saw the amount of money to be made that he got involved".

"I like Jim, but how the fuck could he be of any use to them? From what you say they had it all sewn up".

"They flooded the market with the Isle of Wight gear and a gram of coke went down by a third. It was so cheap that kids who had been sniffing glue were smoking dope, dope smokers were sniffing coke, and your coke-heads were doing heroin. Drugs became affordable to everyone, not just your rock star set".

"So where does Jimmy come in"?

"That shit didn't last forever. They needed a safe way to get more into the country. You've got your small time dealers who are happy with the contents of a couple Johnnies full that come into the country shoved up some bird's fanny, but Roger and Dave were supplying every dealer within a fifty mile radius of London. What do you know about Afghanistan, Vinny"?

"Not a lot. Just what I saw on Rambo III: a load of rag-heads riding around on horses and fighting the Russians".

"That's right. Well the war ended in eighty-eight. Let me tell you a few more facts about Afghanistan: they are the largest producer of cannabis and opium, heroin is made from opium and the Russians love their heroin. The heroin leaves northern Afghanistan through Central Asia and on to Russia. Dave knew all this because he was very friendly with a Russian hooker who defected from Russia because she pissed off some nasty Mafia boss".

"Yeah, I've met her. Her name's Nadine and there's another Russian bird there now called Nadia. Jimmy's been driving her about".

"He would do. Believe it or not, Jimmy's key to the whole operation".

"Bollocks".

"Yeah, it's hard to believe, but he's got the perfect set up for bringing the drugs in: he's been importing a container full of old scooters every four months from India. India borders Pakistan, and Pakistan borders Afghanistan. Even that fat useless fucker, Ken, is in on it. All of them except you. They've treated you like a mug. Yeah, they threw you a bone by giving you a share in the club, but that's nothing compared to what they're getting. Talk about take the piss – Dave's even making money out of you while you drive his tarts about".

I sat there in complete shock I couldn't take it all in. What she was saying all added up, but it still didn't make sense. Again, I was about to get up and walk out, when the buzzer on the intercom went off. She went over to it, held her finger on it and said,

"About time. Come up". She opened the door and Ray walked in.

"Sorry I'm late. Have I missed all the fun? By the look on your face Vinny, it would appear so".

"Yes, I've been filling Vinny in and he's pretty much up to speed. I was saving the best for when you got here".

"Don't look so gutted Vinny. You weren't the only one to get mugged off – we did as well. Don't get mad, get even. If we work together on this we can turn it round in our favour".

It was the way Ray looked over to Doreen and smirked and the way she smiled back that made me feel uneasy. Ray walked over to the decanter and poured a drink. I got up to leave 'cos I'd heard enough. I couldn't take it all in. I'd taken a couple of steps when Ray turned round.

"Don't leave yet Vinny. You haven't heard the best bit".

"And what's that then"?

"How we get even".

"What 'ave you gotta get even for"?

"Plenty mate. I was well in with Jack Warren until Jimmy came along. I was running the best nightclub in London, The Ritzy, and I was making all the right contacts and paving the way to a fortune then the next thing I know Jack's got rid of me and I ended up running some shit-hole club in Southend. It set me back years".

"So what's the master plan then"

"We've already started: Rudy was the first, so you can expect to see him back out of retirement very soon; Dave's next and that's where you come in".

"Nah, fuck off. You keep me out of your little crusade".

"How do you fancy about five or six grand a week"? I couldn't resist that kinda money.

"Go on. I'm interested".

"We've been looking into Dave's escort agency and we reckon, on an average night, he's covering about thirty hours. Would that be right"?

"I've not worked it out".

"Well, let's do some figures shall we? On a Monday, Tuesday, Wednesday and Thursday, how many girls has he got in"?

"About ten a night, Friday and Saturday is thirty to forty, and Sunday is more like twenty".

"So, ten girls during the week. How many hours would each girl do"?

"Depends on the girl. Some do ten, some five or six, but none of them do less than three".

"Alright then, let's say they average five each, which is fifty hours at thirty quid an hour he gets... which is"? Before I could answer Doreen came up with the figure.

"Fifteen hundred. Times that by four, which equals six grand. Let's say Friday, Saturday and Sunday you double the hours because you've said you get forty girls in. You can safely say Dave's clearing ten grand a week."

"So my five or six grand a week estimate was way out. It looks like you'll clear about ten". Ray was pretty pleased with himself about that.

"I have been thinking of starting up my own agency. I've never really trusted Dave 'cos he's been a little too much involved with Roger for my liking and, from what you've been saying, my gut feeling's been right. But Dave's not just gonna roll over and give me his fucking business".

"No, course he ain't. You leave Dave to us. All you've got to do is set up a rival agency called Sugar and Spice Escorts and when it's been running a couple of weeks, Dave's agency will be shut down and all his girls, along with their punters, will come over to yours".

"And how you gonna get Dave shut down"?

"Let's just say Dave has been a lucky fucker over the years and it's about time he done a spell at Her Majesty's Pleasure. You, me, we've all done time, so a few years won't hurt him".

"You've got it all sussed out, ain't yer"?

"Yes we have. The office is above Unit 16 on the New Trading Estate in Stevenage and the ads are booked in all the local papers for next week. All you need are a few girls and drivers to get it going and you can leave the rest to us".

"So why don't you do it yourself? Why give it to me? What's

in it for you"?

"Like I said earlier, you're the only family I've got. Besides you'll come in handy when we decide to sort Jack and Roger out".

"So Vinny, have we got a deal"? asked Ray.

"I'll have to think about it". Doreen's face looked like thunder. She was not happy.

"There's nothing to think about Vinny. I've given you the facts. You walk away from this offer and you'll be going down with them, so have we got a deal or not"?

"Yeah, I'm in". I knew better than to refuse Doreen when she was in one of her black moods. Ray was all business though:

"Good. Start ringing around and get everything up and running for next Thursday".

I left the apartment totally confused. I didn't trust Doreen and it was spooky how similar she was to Mike. I had a bad feeling about it all. I could believe all the stuff with Dave, Roger and Jack, but Jimmy? How could I be so wrong about him? I really thought he was a mate, so I went round to see him straight away.

"All right Vinny? Come in mate. Fucking 'ell, I don't see yer for weeks, then I see yer twice in one day".

"I felt bad rushing off earlier, but I was meeting Doreen".

"Yeah, I was gonna ask yer what was that all about. I didn't think you had fuck all to do with her"?

"I don't. It was just some business to do with my old man from way back".

"So, how's things? You're not missing the club then"?

"Nah, it's not really my thing. I can't handle dealing with piss-heads and all that fucking loud music. How you doing, Jim? You seem a bit better. We all thought you'd top yourself when Tracy died".

"I come close mate, but Judy helped me a lot".

"Jim, if Tracy hadn't died what were your plans for the future"?

"We were stashing as much cash as we could then, when the kids grew up and left, we were gonna sell up and buy a place in Portugal".

"So you've got a fair bit stashed 'ave yer"?

"Enough mate. Why"?

"No reason".

I was there for about an hour and a few things he said did tally up with what Doreen said: he mentioned about the bike shop and importing scooters from India and he was really fucking cagey about how much cash he had.

Thursday came around and I managed to poach five girls and three drivers from Dave and we were kept busy all night. The next day Dave rang me and wanted to meet up so I went round to see him. I thought he'd be pissed off, but instead he and Bunny were fine. They thought me setting up a rival agency was a good idea and they wanted to help me because there were times when they ran out of girls and, rather than loose the punter, they could pass them on to me and vice versa. I said it was fine because I knew he was getting fucked over by Ray and Doreen and, by us still being mates, it took me out the frame when it did eventually go tits up.

It didn't take long for Ray and Doreen to set him up. They paid some junkie kid who was fifteen to go for an interview with Dave. Everyone except Bunny knew that Dave's interview involved a two hour session in a cheap hotel room. Dave loved young girls and, needless to say, she passed with flying colours. The first night she was at Dave's office she planted enough coke to send him down for five years. Lucky for Dave that when the Old Bill raided the office he weren't there. Bunny was and she was nicked straight away and the office was boarded up. There was a warrant out for Dave's arrest and it weren't just for the drugs; it was for sex with a minor, money laundering, and tax evasion. He was deep in the shit and on the run. He turned up at my gaff and I told him to fuck off so he went round to Jim's.

CHAPTER 6

RUDY'S STORY

"Come in Dave. What are you looking all stressed about"?

"Get us a drink Jim and I'll tell yer".

"What do yer want, a beer"?

"You got something stronger"?

"There's a JD. Get that down yer. Now what's going on"?

"Fucking Old Bill are after me, ain't they"?

"What you done now"?

"More like what I ain't done. They raided the office and found about ten wraps of coke".

"So what? Any of them birds could have left that there".

"Yeah, you're right, but they want me for money laundering, tax evasion, living off immoral earnings, and the icing on the cake is shagging an under-age girl".

"Fucking 'ell, Dave! What yer doing shagging kids"

"I ain't a fucking nonce, Jim. It was one bird and she said she was eighteen".

"Jesus, you are in the shit. You could be looking at ten years for that little lot".

"Ten years? I can't do that! You gotta help me get out the country".

"Where was you thinking of"?

"I don't know. What about Brazil? That's where Ronnie Biggs

ended up and they couldn't touch him there".

"You can't just jump on a plane to Brazil; you don't know fuck all about the place. I tell yer what – why don't you go over to Rudy's place in Jamaica? It'll give yer time to think".

"Fucking great idea. Give him a bell".

Dave was in a right state, he was a good mate, but I didn't want him at my place. If the Old Bill found him here I'd be going down with him. We tried ringing Rudy for a couple of days, but couldn't get hold of him so I suggested to Dave to just go.

"Look, he ain't answering. Just go".

"What do you mean "just go"? How the fuck am I gonna find him"?

"The same way I did".

"I didn't know you'd been there".

"Yeah, I spent a couple of weeks there with Tracy".

"Well, come with me. What have you got here"?

"I can't just drop everything and fuck off".

"Why not"?

Dave had a point. Steven was running The Punch Bowl and Ken was looking after the shop, so I thought why not? I could do with a holiday. It took us a couple of days to sort the flights out and get Dave a fake passport, then we had our cases packed ready to go and we was just waiting for Bunny to pick us up when there was a knock on the door. I opened it and who was standing there with a big grin on his face? Only fucking Rudy!

"What the fuck are you doing 'ere"?

"That's no way to greet me man. I've come to see my friend".

"Come in". He sauntered into the living room, where Dave was just as surprised to see him.

"What the fuck are you doing 'ere"?

"What is this? Some kinda new white boy greeting? And what are all these cases for? Are you going somewhere"?

"Yeah. We were coming to see you"!

"Get away man. That's great! Here I am". This was obviously getting to Dave, as his hope for a hideout had just turned up on the doorstep.

"No it ain't. Why aren't you sitting on a beach with a little umbrella in a fucking cocktail, chilling out"?

"It's a long, long story man". Rudy's stories are always worth listening to, so I settled in for a good one.

"Well we're not going anywhere now, so make yourself comfortable. We've got all the time in the world".

When I'd opened the door and seen Rudy, he looked terrible. His hair always looked a mess with all them tangled dreadlocks, but he was normally a snappy dresser. I weren't even too sure what he was wearing, but it looked like some sort of uniform and boy did he smell bad. Dave weren't too keen either and didn't bother being polite about it,

"Jesus, Rudy! You fucking stink".

"So would you if you'd spent three weeks hiding on a damn cargo ship", Rudy jibed back. I didn't like where this was going and I told him so,

"Something tells me I ain't gonna like what you're gonna tell me, am I"?

"It all started..."

Before Rudy could continue, Dave got up, opened the window and said,

"Right, before you go any further, get upstairs and have a shower. I'll put some clean clothes and a bin liner outside the door".

"While I make myself nice and shiny is there any chance you can provide me with some food"?

Rudy went upstairs to get cleaned up, singing in the shower like he didn't have a care in the world.

"So what do yer reckon then? It don't look good does it? He goes out on a plane first class and comes back on a fucking banana boat like his Mum and Dad did".

"One thing's for sure: we ain't going to Jamaica, so I'll get us a Kentucky and some more beers in".

Half an hour later I got back to find Rudy sitting in my favourite chair, puffing on the biggest joint I've ever seen, while Dave was pouring himself another JD.

"You can't smoke that shit in 'ere".

"Sorry man. I was forgetting the little lady don't like the weed. Where is that lovely girl of yours"?

"She died about six months ago".

"Shit man. No way".

"Yeah some drunk run her off the road", Dave chipped in.

"I'm sorry to hear that. She was a lovely girl... and what about you, Dave? Where's the lovely Bunny"?

"She's still about, but I think she's had enough of me 'cos I ain't seen her since the Old Bill have been looking for me".

Rudy tried to take it all in at once, but struggled.

"What's going on man? Jim, why didn't you tell me about Tracy"?

"I've been in a pretty bad way since she died and I've only just started to sort myself out".

"Right. And why are the police after you, Dave? What you been getting up to"?

"Don't worry about what I've been up to", said Dave "You was gonna tell us why you're back here".

"Yeah, Rudy. What's going on"?

"I'm not too sure man – I thought you might know something".

"What the fuck are you talking about"?

"Back when we brought the gear back from the island and we sorted everything out with the brothers and the police, who else, apart from those who took part, knew that I survived the raid and went home"?

"It was just us", I said, Why?"

"Because some bad arse, mother fucking brothers back home knew a hell of a lot about what went down back then".

"What exactly has happened back home"? Dave demanded.

"Well, after the big celebration at the club, I flew off to Jamaica the next morning. When I got back home I spent five weeks chilling on the beach with the little umbrella in the fucking cocktail, but I got bored and I bought myself a small hotel outside Montego Bay. I changed my name to Floyd and I was doing really well".

"When you say hotel, do you mean some sort of shitty little guest house"?

"Nah, it was really nice", I stuck up for him.

"It had a five star rating and we had the big holiday companies sending people over. Jamaica is a beautiful country and I used to give the guests tours in my mini bus. I took them to the crocodile farm that was in the James Bond film Live and Let Die, I took them to the Dunns River Falls and, for the really adventurous, I took them along the North of the island and down through The Blue Mountains and in to Kingston to see Bob Marley's house".

"Sounds like you had it good". Dave was clearly jealous, but Rudy weren't actually tellin' us what happened.

"Good? It was perfect man. And in the evening I'd sing in my band".

"So what 'appened then? Why 'ave you turned up on my doorstep looking like shit"?

"One of the brothers who got wasted in the shoot-out had a son called Winston. Now, Winston searched high and low back then to try and find out who set his Dad and uncles up. He gave up after a few years and took over where his Dad left off. Then, six months ago, Winston started buying his gear from a big-shot dealer who owns some clubs and that club owner starts telling

Winston exactly what went down back then".

"Don't tell me it was Roger", I groaned.

"No, that's what I thought, but it wasn't Roger. Anyway, it wasn't long before Winston was on a plane to Kingston. He came over to find a safe way of getting high quality coke over to England and also to get me. The Yardies in Kingston were using drug mules to smuggle the coke over, but too many were getting caught. It didn't take long for Winston to track me down. He woke me up one night with a pistol stuck in my face".

"How the fuck did you get out of that one"? asked Dave.

"I turned it all around and blamed you lot of course, but Winston weren't convinced so I offered to help him get his gear off the island. I had the perfect set up: a respectable hotel with no shortage of British holiday makers all year round. I knew exactly when they were out, I had keys for their rooms, and I knew where they lived back in England because I looked after their passports. When they were out for the day we would go to their rooms and stash as much gear as we could in the lining of their cases. If we couldn't do that, we would just slip a couple of packs in their cases just before they left for the airport. When they got back home Winston's boys were waiting to relieve them of their luggage".

"And that worked"? snorted Dave.

"Not always. That's why I'm back here".

"So what went wrong then"? I asked.

"We only went and stashed two packs of high grade coke in the Chief Superintendent's case and, instead of him going straight home, he stayed at a hotel in Heathrow and opened his case... "Me and Dave were a bit pissed, so we could see the funny side of it, but poor Rudy was nearly in tears as he was telling us.

"The first I knew about it was when I arrived back from a day at the bay and there were policemen everywhere, so I slipped away and disappeared into the mountains for a few weeks".

"I didn't know there was mountains over there".

"Mountains, forest... Jamaica is a beautiful country, but when you're wanted by the police the mountains are the only place you safe. I couldn't live in the mountains forever though 'cos there was some serious bad brothers living off the land. It was time for Floyd to leave, so I has me a plan: I became friends with a nasty man called Gregory".

"And what did Gregory do"? I asked.

"He one bad arse mother fucker. He gun down his rival's wife and children and not even his own want anything to do with that man".

"And you became friends with him"? Dave was shocked.

"I just needed to gain his trust enough to get him to come back with me to the hotel. Gregory liked me and I convinced him that I had enough money and the right contacts to get us off the island and over to England".

"Jesus! You ain't bought him with yer"? I couldn't 'ave that kinda guy in my house.Rudy leaned back in the chair, took a big puff of his joint and laughed as he said,

"No, man. I blew his damn brains out".

"Hilarious", said Dave. "Why did you do that"?

"Gregory was a bad man; he had it coming to him. Floyd needed to disappear, so when we got back to the hotel I gathered up all my gold jewellery, left the safe door open, and I shot Gregory. Gregory was my height and build, so I then burn the place down and slip away. I bought myself a one way ticket on the first cargo ship bound for England".

"How much did that cost yer"? Dave wanted to know.

"Four gold chains and all of my rings. I have nothing left, but Floyd is now dead and Rudy is alive and kicking".

"So the Old Bill in Jamaica think you're dead"? I checked.

"Yeah man. Is I one clever mother or what"?

Dave was deep in thought for a minute, before he asked the crucial question,

"Hang on a minute. You went to Jamaica and became Floyd

because you set up Winston's old man and uncles. Correct me if I'm wrong, but when Rudy reappears isn't Winston gonna come looking for yer again"?

"Yeah, man. That is a problem I need to figure out, but until I do I can chill with you guys".

"I don't think so. From the sound of it this Winston ain't a silly fucker and someone who we don't know yet is feeding him info about you. When he finds out you're back on the scene this will be the first place he comes looking. It's bad enough you being 'ere, Dave. I don't need a bunch of trigger-happy fucking Yardies turning up".

"Jim, you're not turning me away are you? How would you feel, man, if you did turn up at my place and I turned you away"?

"He's got a point Jim".

"Alright, alright. You can stay, but only for a few days".

"Nice one Jim. I'll be no problem, trust me man. So Dave, why are you running? what you been up to"?

"Like you, I was doing alright 'til someone set me up".

"That's right. I remember you were pimping out girls".

"Was I, bollocks. I was running an escort agency and there's a big fucking difference".

"You was doing alright then"?

"Alright? I was clearing anywhere between ten and fifteen grand a week before this young bird rings up and asks for an interview. She said she'd worked from a flat so I assumed she was old enough. I waited till I got two more for interviews and I booked my usual room at that motel on the motorway".

"So you interview the girls in a hotel room? You dirty bastard", Rudy grinned.

"I don't shag 'em all".

I couldn't resist butting in at that point,

"No, but he did that one and she was fifteen"!

Rudy roared with laughter.

"Fucking jail bait, man. You fool"!

"I didn't know, did I"?

"So that's why the police chase you"?

"Along with the fact he ain't paid any tax and the twelve grams of Charlie they found at the office". This was fun.

"Twelve grams? You dick, man. You don't leave that shit lying around".

"I ain't fucking daft. Someone planted it there".

"Man, look at us. We on the run and you lost that sweet lady. What the fuck is going on? How are the others doing"?

"Charlie and Ron ain't doing too well either. Ken's alright though. In fact, he's turned the shop around now his boy's working with him, and Judy's got herself a bed and breakfast place down in Brighton".

"I wasn't too sure about that Ken bloke. He didn't like me 'cos of the colour of my skin".

"Yeah, Ken ain't a great lover of any foreigners. Don't take it personal. He was alright in the end though. He started to warm to yer a bit". I stuck up for Ken 'cos he'd been a good mate to me.

"And what about the bad boy – Vinny"?

"He's doing great. In fact he's taken over where I left off", answered Dave.

"And do you not think that's strange"?

"Vinny's alright. He wouldn't do anything". I stuck up for another mate.

"No hang on a minute Jim, Rudy's got a point. Vinny knew exactly how I worked with the girls and he had the perfect chance to stash that gear".

"Nah, I'm not 'aving none of it. Vinny wouldn't do that".

"You gotta look at every possibility Jim. Someone set the man up".

Rudy had a point. In fact, I never really thought Rudy had a lot up top, but pulling that little disappearing act off in Jamaica was a stroke of genius. Now all he had to do was get this Winston off his back. We talked well in to the night and had a right laugh talking about things we'd been up to. Rudy was a real character and I think that was the first time I'd laughed properly since Tracy's death. Rudy stayed a few days and then we all went down to stay at Judy's in Brighton. I went down on my scooter and Dave and Rudy went by train.

CHAPTER 7

KIDNAPPING JACK'S DAUGHTER

It had been eight weeks since Dave's agency was shut down and you wouldn't believe the money I was making. The amounts we estimated round Doreen's were well out; I was clearing fifteen grand a week. The agency never closed so it was a twenty-four hour job. I never told Doreen exactly what I was making. In fact, I stashed half of everything I made and the only one who knew the exact amount was Bunny. Dave was still on the run from the Old Bill and Bunny was twiddling her thumbs doing nothing, so she helped me run things. We were spending a lot of time together and I got to know her really well. Actually, I fancied the arse off her, but the worrying thing was that it wasn't just a physical attraction – I really liked her. Everyone knew about Dave and Bunny's relationship, but it was only Dave's side of things we got to hear. Based on some of the things I'd heard about them and what they got up to, there's no way I could be in that sort of relationship, so I thought I'd try and get her side of things.

"So what's gonna happen when the Old Bill finally catch up with Dave then"?

"I don't really care. Me and Dave are finished".

"You're joking. You've been together fucking ages".

"Yeah, about thirty years, but I've had enough now; him shagging that young bird was the final straw".

"Why's that such a big deal? I thought you two were always up to that sort of thing"?

"Yeah, that's what everyone thinks and that's what we let 'em think, but the truth is I was never really into it all. It was just Dave and I never denied it because it was my way of keeping my pride intact. I didn't want people thinking I was this poor little mug stuck indoors while Dave was out shagging whatever he could get his hands on".

"So what was so bad about him shagging that bird? Is it because of her age"?

"Yeah, that's part of it – how can I compete with that I'm forty five? The other thing is: I don't like being lied to. He promised he wouldn't shag the girls at the agency and now I've found out he's shagged most of them. No wonder we were only getting it on once a week. Mind you, I'm glad we were 'cos when I found out what he'd been up to I was dead scared in case he'd given me something. I got myself checked out at the clinic last week though, and thankfully I'm all clear".

"Thirty years is a fucking long time. There must have been something special between yer. I mean, you must have loved each other".

"I don't think we did really. When we started going out with each other neither one of us was looking for love".

"Why's that then"?

"We've all known each other for years; me, Dave, Ron, Charlie, Judy and Jimmy, we all went to the same school. I always fancied Dave 'cos he was a laugh, but he was always getting into trouble and he never really noticed me. In fact, he weren't really that into girls until he was fourteen. His Dad was never in and we all used to hang out at his house, where his Dad had this really cool record collection. One day he asked just me back to his house and I thought he was gonna ask me out. We started drinking his Dad's gin and playing records and he put his arm round me and started kissing me. I pushed him away and said he'd have to ask me out first so he did. I let him touch me up a bit but he was really getting carried away and the things he wanted to do were disgusting, so I left. I was really shocked and the next day at school I told him I didn't want to go out with him no more".

"So he was a dirty fucker even at school"?

"Yeah he was".

"Jimmy used to fancy you as well didn't he"?

"Yeah, bless him. You had two extremes with Dave and Jimmy. Dave wanted to do things that weren't even in the Karma Sutra and Jimmy was all gooey-eyed and in love, bless him".

"Didn't he get off with you once"?

"Yeah, in Brighton when we were Mods. He'd been following me around all weekend and when the bloke I was with got off with someone else we had a bit of fun, but poor Jimmy thought I felt the same as him and I didn't. Anyway he got nicked and when we got back home I saw Dave down The Goldhawk Club and he asked me if I fancied a bit of fun. I remembered what he wanted to do to me at fourteen and I thought I had nothing to lose. So you see, neither one of us was looking for love. It was always a relationship based on crazy fun".

"Didn't you feel bad about Jimmy"?

"This sounds terrible, but no; I didn't give a toss. I felt a bit guilty when he lost the plot and ended up inside".

"So what 'appened? You and Dave eventually fell in love I suppose..."

"Looking back, I don't think it was ever love. What Jimmy and Tracy had was love. I sometimes looked at them and I was really envious of Tracy, 'cos me and Dave were more like good mates. Still, I haven't left it too late to find love".

"Jimmy's free now".

"Nah he's not my type".

"So what's your type now"?

"Someone who's strong, successful, that ain't carrying any baggage like kids, and they've gotta be handsome. Do yer know

anyone who fits the bill"?
She looked me straight in the eye as she said it and leaned back in her chair and smiled. I was amazed at her honesty and I can see how everyone assumed what she was like I could feel myself starting to sweat I was about to tell her I fitted the bill, but before I could, she said,

"And what about you? You're a good looking bloke, so why ain't you found someone"?

"I've just not met the right one yet. The trouble is, working down the club, all the girls I ended up with were thick as shit. One night stands mostly. Don't get me wrong; they've all been stunners, but it ain't just about looks is it"?

"So, are you looking for love Vinny"?

"Yeah, I am. What's the point in 'aving all this money if you ain't got anyone to share it with"?
She knew I fancied her, she was just playing games with me, I couldn't make out whether she fancied me or not so I thought, "fuck it I'll give it a go".

"I'm looking for love alright. In fact, I think I've found it".

"Who's the lucky girl then"?

You, and you know it".

"Of course I know it! Everyone's noticed that you can't keep your eyes off me, so why haven't you made a move before"?

"Well, it's not right is it making a move on your mate's bird, is it"?

"As I said, me and Dave are finished".

"Yeah, I know that now".

"So when are you gonna take me on our first date then"?

"We can go out tonight if you want? Ring Debbie and Amanda and get them to cover the shift".
I dropped Bunny off home and arranged to pick her up again at nine. I'd decided to take her to a casino. I was starting to feel really bad though; not only had I nicked Dave's business, but then I'd nicked his Missus. The problem was that I really liked her. I'd

never felt like this about anyone. If I was looking at her as just another shag then I wouldn't give a bollock if she found out I was behind Dave losing the club, but if two, three months or even years down the line we're still together and she finds out, I didn't know if I would be able to handle losing her. The other thing that was bothering me was she must have known about Dave, Jimmy and Roger keeping all that money to themselves and cutting me out of the loop. It made me wonder if she was only looking at me as a meal ticket 'cos Dave was gonna end up inside. I decided to take her out, have a good time and quiz her a bit more in the office the next day, when it was quiet.

The night went really well. She looked stunning in a long black dress with a real fur jacket. She was like a film star. She was no stranger to a roulette wheel and I can see why Dave needed so much money – we ended up doing about five grand. At the end of the night I dropped her off home, but there was no invite in for coffee, just a peck on the cheek and a thank you.. We got to the office the next morning at seven and the night shift were sitting around in the office as usual, filling us in on the night's events. Bunny was the same as normal and there was no mention of our night out. Then, when the night shift girls left, she leaned over my desk, kissed me on the cheek and said,

"Thanks for a great night".

"That's alright. It was a laugh weren't it"?

"You weren't too disappointed that I didn't ask you in then"?

"Course I fucking was. You looked stunning"!

"Aah, poor Vinny. There's plenty of time for that though".

"So, you wanna do it again then"?

"Yeah, I do. The thing is I really like you, but I don't know much about you and I don't want another relationship based on lust alone. I need to get to know you much better".

I wanted to get to know her better as well, so I thought I'd see if I could find out if she knew what Dave had been up to.

"You and Dave have been doing this for a few years now. You must 'ave a few bob stashed".

"Don't make me laugh. You've seen the way Dave spends money".

"Yeah, I've seen the way you do as well. You done five grand on that roulette wheel."

"You're not a tight arse, are you Vinny"?

"Nah, course I ain't. It was worth every penny seeing how much fun you was 'aving".

"Don't get me wrong, I like my designer clothes and I spend a fortune on shoes and bags, but Dave's in a different league to me. That new motor he's got set him back eighty grand, he's got his boat down in Dorset and we spent a fortune on first class travel and posh hotels. We were shit with money and that's why he's hiding away with Rudy at Jimmy's place. He ain't only got the Old Bill after him; the tax man wants him as well".

"I didn't know Rudy's back! No-one told me."

"No-one's meant to know. Until he's got to the bottom of what went wrong in Jamaica, he's keeping his head down".

"I thought he was doing alright out there. I know he stopped dealing".

"He was. I don't know the full story, but someone fucked him up just like Dave".

"You reckon Dave was set up then"?

"Course he was. No-one leaves that amount of coke lying around and the most the girls have is a couple of wraps at a time. Why would that kid go to the Old Bill? Dave didn't rape her; she knew exactly what she was doing".

"So you got any idea who's behind it then"?

"Not sure, but it's either Ray or Roger".

"Why's that then? I thought they were all in it together".

"In what? What did you think they were into"?

"Drugs, dealing, supplying… you know".

"I know Dave weren't. He didn't want nothing to do with

it. They approached him at the same time as they tried getting Jimmy involved. No, the only drugs Dave got was a couple of grams a week for us. Ray's the one running the show when it comes to drugs. He wanted to get involved with the agency, but Dave weren't interested. He even offered to buy us out on the condition we didn't start another one".

"What did he offer you"

"Two hundred grand".

"Fucking hell. Why didn't you take it"?

"Because it was nowhere near enough. We would have done that in a few months".

"So what would they have gained by setting him up"?

"With Dave banged up and his agency shut down, Ray could then set up another one. That's why Dave was pleased you set up Sugar and Spice; he can trust you and he knew you could work together".

"So why hasn't Ray set up an agency then, if he was behind it"?

"That's what we can't figure out. It must be because you've got this place, so I'd watch your back".

"Yeah, I will do. I ain't gonna make the same mistakes Dave did. in fact, I've got an accountant coming in later to sort things out so the tax man's kept away".

Fucking 'ell. How bad did I feel? Dave really liked me and trusted me and I'd done exactly what he was scared Ray was gonna do. Something didn't add up though 'cos if Ray wanted an agency so bad, why had he and Doreen given it to me? After getting to know Bunny, I was sure she wasn't fucking stupid. If Dave had a couple of million in a Swiss bank account, she'd definitely know about it.

Doreen had set the meeting up with Alex, the accountant, 'cos she said there was some papers I had to sign. When he walked in the office Bunny recognised him straight away. "I know you from somewhere, don't I"?

"I don't think so love".

"Yeah, I do. I never forget a face, but I just can't place you at the moment".

"Well, my name's Alex. What's yours"?

"Bunny".

"Well Bunny, me and Vinny have got lots of boring paperwork to get through, so if you don't mind why don't you go and do your nails or something and leave us alone"?

"You're a right charmer".

"No, I'm not. I'm a fucking good accountant and time's money, so fuck off".

"Oi! Who the fuck do you think you're talking to, you skinny cunt"?

He looked Bunny up and down like she was a piece of shit and said,

"Bunny's your name, ain't it"?

"That's my partner, you fucking twat. Now you've got ten seconds to apologise before I rip your fucking 'ead off".

Alex practically started wetting himself. He tried to dig himself out the hole he had dug.

"I'm very sorry Bunny. I thought you was one of the girls that work here. If you want me to leave, Vinny, perhaps we can do this another time".

"No, stay. Let's get this done, then you can fuck off".

Bunny stayed and Alex pulled four or five documents out of his case.

"Right, I just need you to sign where I've put the crosses in pencil".

Bunny was looking over my shoulder and reading the documents, which were tax documents for companies I hadn't heard of. One of them was a company called DW Holdings, so I asked him what they were.

"I ain't being funny, but what the fuck am I signing"?

"You don't need to know".

Bunny wasn't having any of that,

"Yeah you do,Vinny".

"Those two are tax documents and the other three are registration documents to set up a fake company for you to put the money you make from this place through", Alex gave in.

"Fake company, fake document… do you do this sort of thing often"?

"All the time".

"What if I wanted fake bank statements? Would that be a problem"?

"Not at all".

I signed the documents and he left.

"I know where I've seen him before; it was at Jimmy and Tracy's wedding".

"Fuck me! You've got a good memory. That must have been twenty odd years ago. You sure"?

"Yeah, I told yer, I never forget a face. Especially when it belongs to an obnoxious prick like him. Dave was being his usual self, talking to Tracy, and that arsehole tried chatting me up. He was one of your Dad's mates".

"Was he? I wouldn't know. I had fuck all to do with my old man".

"Vinny, what's going on? Why's one of your Dad's old firm sniffing round here"?

"Look, all I know is he came highly recommended. He's the best at making money disappear from the tax man and turning dodgy money into clean".

Bunny was starting to get suspicious – I could see her mulling it around in her head and she weren't the only one. I was starting to doubt everything Doreen had said about the drugs, and that statement she showed me didn't prove fuck all now I knew how easily Alex knocked out fake documents. And, if Ray wanted Dave's agency so bad, why were they giving it to me? If Doreen weren't my sister then I would have been well worried. Bunny started asking more questions, so I changed the subject and took her out shopping. She loved shopping and I fucking hated it. Over the next four or five weeks we started to really get close. I wanted to tell her about Doreen, but I was scared she'd blow me out 'cos she still really cared about Dave.

Doreen left me alone, but she was constantly there in the back of my mind. I knew she was up to something, but at this stage I didn't want to know what it was because the thing in the front of my mind was Bunny. I'd never felt like that about anyone before.

The day shift at the agency was always quiet, so Bunny only came in Mondays to help me cash up and sort out any problems from the weekend. I couldn't have run the agency without her. She kept the girls in check and kept records of all the regular clients including what they liked and who their favourite girls were. She got on well with the girls and the drivers, but she had a ruthless edge to her. She monitored how many hours each girl did and, if a girl was constantly doing one hour jobs and not extending, they were sacked. She knew Dave was set up so she stopped the girls doing drugs in the office. We didn't give a toss what they got up to with the clients, but the office was a strictly no drugs zone. She even put a sign on the wall saying any girl or driver caught with drugs on them would be sacked. We knew most of the girls had them and a few of the drivers were dealing, but on the odd occasion the Old Bill came sniffing around it just looked good that we were seen to be trying to discourage it. She learnt a lot from how Dave run his agency and she didn't want me making the same mistakes.

It's a good job she did only come in Mondays because I wouldn't have wanted her around when I got a visit from Roger.

"Alright, Vinny? I haven't seen you for a while. How you been doing"?

"I'm good mate. I tell yer what – I'm making a fucking fortune with this place".

"Good. I"m glad to hear it 'cos I want to sell out my share of The Punch Bowl".

"Sit down Roger. Can I get yer a tea or coffee"?

"Coffee; black, no sugar".

"So, why do you want out of the club? We're getting a nice steady income from that place and we don't 'ave to do fuck all now Jimmy's running it".

"We're making fuck all. It's small change now that it's gone from one of the major clubs north of London to a social club for Jimmy's scooter mates. It should have been updated years ago".

"Why didn't we then"?

"To be honest, I lost interest. Not only that, I was making enough money on other things and besides, Jimmy loves that place. It's always been his so it's only right that he should run it".

"If you care so much about Jimmy, why are you offering it to me? I'd become the major shareholder".

"Because I need cash fast and Jimmy's got fuck all. Are you interested or not"?

"Yeah course I am, but I don't get it. Why do you need cash so desperately? I thought you was fucking minted."

Roger sat back in the chair, smiled and said.

"Yeah, that's what everyone thinks. That's what I thought an' all, but I've been well and truly stitched up by that fucker Ray".

"Fuck me! Who would have thought a fucking coke-head like Ray could get one over on you"?

"Trust me: he ain't the brains behind it. I don't know who is, but I will find out. It's gotta be one of Mike's old firm because Alex has been doing the books".

"Doing the books? What do you mean 'doing the fucking books'? You're a fucking drug dealer".

"Listen, mate, gone are the days when you can swan around in a Roller, live in a mansion, have your own private yacht on the Med, along with the villa. Money comes in dirty and blokes like Alex make sure it's cleaned through legit companies".

"I don't get it. You're a lot of things, but you ain't fucking stupid. What 'appened"?

"Well, you know I was running the Rave scene a few years ago? Well, I realised that the big money was in drugs. Your old man was right. Anyway, Ray approached me because he had a few clubs in Southend and we ended up working well together. The kids were popping 'E's like fucking smarties, but the big money was in coke and heroin. It was a high risk, high gain plan to make a few million then fuck off somewhere warm. I've been in this game too long. The big risk was getting the drugs into the country, but Ray had met some Russian hooker and she knew all the right contacts abroad".

"A Russian? I thought all that shit came from South America".

"Yeah, a lot of coke still does, but most of your heroin comes from Russia via Europe. The Russians fucking love their heroin. Anyway, this Russian bird had the contacts and I don't know how Ray done it, but he was bringing in shit loads of the stuff through a legit company. We were making fucking millions and my share was put through a holdings company".

"It weren't DW Holdings by any chance was it"?

"Yeah it was. How the fuck did you know that"?!

"I don't know what the fuck's going on, but I know who does and I'm gonna get to the bottom of it".

"Do you know who owns that company"?

"I've got an idea".

"Well, share that idea with me 'cos they've filtered my money off somewhere else".

"Don't Ray know"?

"He knows alright. I massively underestimated how smart that fucker is, though. He pissed some big time Russian Mafia boss off and guess who's in the frame for it".

"You".

"Yeah, me. That's why I need some cash fast".

"I wish I could help yer, but all I've got is twenty grand. The rest is in DW Holdings".

"You're fucking joking".

"I wish I was now I know what's 'appened to you. Alex set the accounts up when I got this place up and running".

"So Alex is behind all this"?

"No. I know who is, but I ain't saying no more until my arse is in the clear. If I was you I'd keep my head down till I can work it all out".

"Any suggestions where? I can't go back to my place – it's being watched".

"The only place I can think of is Jim's, but it's a case of there's no more room left at the inn. He's got Dave and Rudy there".

"I wondered where Dave had got to, but what's Rudy doing there"?

"Long story apparently, but someone fucked up his retirement plans in Jamaica".

"Give Jim a bell then and we'll see if he's about".

I rung Jim, but he weren't there. He'd took Dave and Rudy down to Brighton to stay at Judy's.

"He's not there. He's in Brighton, staying at Judy's place. He said there's a few spare rooms and they ain't gonna find yer down there. It's perfect".

"Can I take your motor"?

"No. Leave me out of this until I know exactly what's going on. Get your gear together and I'll drop you at the station".

"This is it mate; the shirt on my back and a passport in my

pocket. All I need is some cash".

"Right, let's go. We'll stop off at my place on the way 'cos all the cash is there".

I gave Roger ten grand and dropped him off at the station then I parked up over the lakes to try and get my head round what the fuck was going on. It looked like I was being set up by Doreen, but it didn't make sense. Why go to all that trouble just so she could get her hands on a poxy escort agency? Then I remembered her saying I would be of use to her later. I decided not to tell Roger and the others what was going on until I knew the full story. It was too much for me to take in on my own though, so I decided to tell Bunny and be straight with her from the start because I had a bad feeling this was gonna get very fucking messy. The office was the best place to chat so I sent the three day girls and driver home and switched the phones off.

"Bunny, I had an interesting visit from Roger".

"What's he want"?

"Money. He's on the run".

"Don't trust him, Vinny. I'm sure he had something to do with setting Dave up".

"No, he didn't. He had fuck all to do with it. I know exactly who's behind it all".

"Go on".

"It's my sister, Doreen, and she's used me to do it. I was always gonna set up my own agency as there's enough work out there. You was always running out of girls and drivers—".

"Wait a minute. I didn't think you had anything to do with your sisters after Mike died".

"I didn't, but just before I set up this place Doreen wanted to see me, so I went to see her in this fucking big apartment in London. It must have been worth millions. Anyway, she was telling me that Dave, Jack, Roger and Jimmy were making shit loads of money dealing in drugs".

Bunny started laughing.

"And you believed it"?

"I didn't at first, but she showed me a statement for a foreign account with their names on it and some of the stuff she was saying made sense".

"Like what"?

"Well, she reckoned that they were using Jimmy's bike shop to smuggle the drugs in from India in containers of scooters".

"I can see how you'd think Dave and Roger were into all that but, you know Jimmy's as straight as a die".

"Yeah, I know. I've been fucking stupid, but she sounded so convincing. Anyway, she helped me get this place up and running, then she set Dave up".

"Well, let's go to the Old Bill and tell 'em".

"Tell 'em what? The fact is, he did shag that bird, drugs were found at your place and Dave has been a silly fucker with the money".

"So basically then, you've helped fuck Dave up and you've nicked his business and what am I? The cherry on the fucking cake"? She was not a happy Bunny.

"Yeah, I know that's what it looks like, but it weren't planned like that. I never in a million years thought you'd fancy me".

"So, what do you do now"?

"I don't know. That's why I'm telling you".

"Does Roger know she's behind it"?

"No, not yet. He knows I know who's behind it, but until I find out exactly what she's up to, I thought it best not to say anything. She said I'll be useful to her later".

"You know once you're no use to her she's gonna fuck you up as well".

"I don't think she will. I'm her brother for fuck's sake".

"Don't be so fucking stupid, Vinny. It's obvious what she's doing: it's revenge for what you lot done to Mike. So what, you're her brother? Mike was your Dad, but you still helped screw him. Family values obviously ain't high on the Warren's list of priorities, are they? You hated your Dad, but Doreen loved him so believe me she's got something lined up for you. What about Ken, Ron, Charlie and Jimmy? What's she gonna do to them"?

"Fucking "ell. You're totally right".

"Course I am, but don't you think we better warn them"?

"No, not yet. Chances are she's already done it but they don't know it yet. She's done all this to turn me against them, so I'll play along with the brotherly love thing and see what I can find out. If you tell Roger he could blow it all, so just give me a few days and I'll see what I can do".

I had been dreading telling Bunny in case she felt sorry for Dave and blew me out, but I'm glad I did in the end because she helped me make sense of it all. I rang Doreen to tell her that Roger had been to see me and she wanted to see me that afternoon at five. I drove into London early to miss the rush hour and I got to her place at four. I didn't go up; just sat in my car round the corner to try and calm my nerves because I was shitting myself. I'd only been there about ten minutes and the apartment block door opened and who should walk out, only Ray and that Russian hooker Nadine. That was enough to confirm everything to me. For me to convince Doreen that I was on her side, I would have to revert back to the old Vinny; the nasty bastard Vinny that cut a landlord to ribbons in front of his missus. As I walked into her apartment she was over the other side, pouring herself a drink.

"I'll 'ave one of them while you're there".

"I thought you was a beer drinker Vinny".

"I am, but I'm still a bit stressed with that arsehole Roger coming round".

"What did he want"?

"He wanted cash. He wanted me to buy him out of the Punch Bowl".

"What did you tell him"?

"I told him to go fuck himself".

"And that was it? He didn't say anything else"?

"I didn't give him a chance".

"Good. What about the others? Have you seen any of them"?

"Yeah, and you're right; they've all got their lives mapped out, tossers. Not one of them was interested in me. I haven't seen Dave since he's been on the run, but I can't wait to tell him I've not only nicked his business, but I'm fucking his missus as well".

"Nice. I like your style".

"Yeah, they can all go fuck 'emselves. Who needs mates? Family comes first now. It was them that turned me against Dad, especially Jimmy. I'd like to see him lose it all".

"So, you regret what happened then, with Dad"?

"Course I do. I didn't realise at the time, but they tried to make it look like I set him up, but it was me trying to help him. I didn't know till the last minute that they switched the drop to The Punch Bowl. I had nothing to do with it".

We talked for hours and she was really starting to thaw out and loosen up a bit, so I told her story after story about how I got great pleasure beating the shit out of the punters who treated the girls a bit rough. None of it was true of course; we very rarely got any hassle from punters, but she was loving it. She even asked me to tell her in great detail how I sliced that landlord up and the more graphic I got, the more she liked it. She was drinking a lot and really opening up to me.

"Dad should never have stuck you in that club with a prat like Jimmy. You would have been a valuable asset to the firm".

"Well, I tried, but I guess he never got over Mum's death and he always blamed me".

"I know. I tried on numerous occasions to talk him round".

"All I wanted was a chance to prove myself. I fucking hated working in that club".

"If you want a chance to prove yourself, I'll give you a chance. I said at our first meeting that you would come in useful and now it's time to see. Setting up them mugs was easy. The one I'm gonna have trouble with is uncle Jack".

"I know you've sorted Rudy and Dave out, but what about the others"?

"The reason Roger wanted cash so desperately is he's got some very nasty Russians after him and they'll be disposing of Ken, Steven and Jimmy too. The Russians get very pissed off when someone tries muscling in on their drug trade and the beauty of it is the idiots haven't got a clue. I've made millions and it's all down to them giving me a constant supply of high grade heroin."

"I don't get it. You said they were the ones dealing".

"I only told you that to get you on side. I didn't know you was well on your way to going out on your own anyway. It was us setting them up".

"Who's us"?

"Me and Ray. they're bringing it in through the bike business and they don't even know it".

"How did you manage that then"?

"It was a bit of a fluke really. Ray has always liked his foreign hookers; the dirty bastard was always in Amsterdam or Thailand. He started seeing this Russian hooker called Nadine and she told him all about the drug trade. Ray was dealing at the time with Roger, but it was mainly 'E's to kids at raves and they wanted to start dealing with the harder stuff. Problem was, they didn't have a reliable source abroad and, even if they did, the hard part was getting it over here".

"And that was where Jimmy's bike shop came in"?

"Yeah, it was a real stroke of luck. That useless, fat fucker, Ken, owed a lot of money and I bought his debt. I wanted to lean on him and watch him squirm then eventually we would have disposed of him, but then he told us all about a regular container of old scooters that he was bringing into the country from India. Ray had a chat with his Russian friend and it turns

money".

As she was describing what she'd do to Jack's daughter she was really savouring every thought. She really was one fucking sick bitch."So, if Jack signs on the dotted line, that's it? End of story"?

"Yes. End of story. Everyone paid the price for killing Dad. Vinny, you can only take revenge so far and I don't want to end up all bitter and twisted. It'll start to show on my pretty face and you wouldn't want that would you"?

I started to feel really uncomfortable as she looked me up and down, taking a big sip of her drink. She smiled and said,

"It's a shame we're related.We'd make a great couple, wouldn't we"?

I didn't answer her, but the thought of it made me feel like puking, so I got back onto the subject of Jack's daughter.

"So, when do you want me to get Helen"?

"Tomorrow night at the club, you'll offer to drive her home, but instead you'll take her to the unit.We'll do the rest".

I left at about two in the morning. It was really heavy shit and I didn't go to sleep. I just sat there thinking how I was gonna sort it all out.The good thing was, I'd done enough to convince the sick bitch I was on her side. I was tired and drained and I needed to talk to Bunny, so I went straight round to her place.

"Well, how did you get on"?

"It's not good. Ken, Jimmy, Roger and even young Steven are on borrowed time".

"What do you mean 'borrowed time'"?

I told Bunny the whole story about how Doreen and Ray had set them up with the Russians and we spent ages trying to come up with a solution. If we went to the Old Bill then would we all get done. The fact is, Dave did do what they want him for, Ken Steven and Jimmy have been importing shit loads of heroin and dope, and with Jimmy's past record, they'd lock him up and throw away the key. Bunny suggested we go to the Russians and tell them about Doreen, but how do you find a load of Russian gangsters? I mean, it's not like you can look them up in the fucking Yellow Pages, and even if we did find them they weren't gonna give a shit who'd been bringing that shit into the country as long as they cut the supply route off. I was fucked. I couldn't get my brain in gear and Bunny was coming up with all the ideas. Some of them were good, but some were fucking stupid like everyone fucking off to Brazil and living in the sun.

"You never said what she had planned for Ron and Charlie".

"No, she never mentioned them. I suppose they're a bit insignificant".

"They were still in on it. And what about Jack"? As she mentioned Jack she sprung into life.

"Jack! He's the only one who can sort this mess out. He's well in with the Old Bill; it was him that sorted the last lot out".

"Exactly, and that's why he wouldn't have fuck all to do with it. He made it clear to Jimmy last time that he's all out of favours".

"What if you bullshit him and tell him the Russians are after him as well"?

"Leave it out. He ain't fucking stupid and in any case, all he'll do is get his copper mate involved, so we might as well go to the Old Bill ourselves".

Bunny was spot on. Jack could easily sort it all out, but if I went to him and told him Doreen's plan he'd just take Helen and deal with Doreen, he wouldn't give a shit about us, so that's why I decided to go along with Doreen and grab Helen. Doreen was capable of anything, so I wanted to get Bunny away until I sorted it out.

"Look Bunny, I've got an idea, but I need to know you're safe, so go down to Judy's place and I'll come down Sunday. Don't say anything to the others".

I dropped Bunny at the station and went back home to get ready. I got to the club at eight and Helen got there at about nine. She was a lovely looking girl and she was 'aving a great time. She was spending a lot of time with Steven, so I went over to have a chat with him. It turns out that he was going out with her. I've never had a lot to do with Steve in the past, but he seemed like a really nice bloke. You can imagine how bad I felt then. Not only was I kidnapping his bird, but I knew he could walk out here and get blown away by some nutty fucking Russian with a Kalashnikov. I didn't have time to tell him the whole story, but I told him he's gotta leave first thing in the morning and take his dad with him down to Judy's in Brighton. He was well confused and obviously worried, but he said he would. I managed to get Helen away from Steven long enough to tell her that Jack had a crash in his car and I'd take her to the hospital. The factory unit I was taking her to was en route, so when I turned off the main road I didn't have to explain too much. I just stared straight ahead and kept going, not listening to her questions. When I turned into the industrial estate, the shutter was open so I drove straight in. As soon as I stopped, two of Doreen's heavies pulled her out the car, screaming and kicking, and took her to a room. Doreen stood there smiling at me.

"Well done. You can go now and leave the rest to us".

As I got back in my car I could hear Helen screaming out to me and I felt like shit.

CHAPTER 8

BRIGHTON – BUNNY'S STORY

The train journey to Brighton took a couple of hours and I spent the whole time worrying about Vinny. When he came round to me after seeing Doreen, I was gonna tell him I was pregnant, but he was so tired and stressed that I didn't know how he'd react. I hadn't been going out with him long, so I didn't know how he felt about kids. I knew he thought the world of me and I liked him in a way I never did with Dave. He was a great bloke, but he weren't the brightest spark and I couldn't see how he could sort the mess out with Doreen. He needed help and I thought the others should know, but I'd promised not to say anything. Besides, I had to break it to Dave that we were definitely over.

Jimmy had arranged to pick me up from the station. When I saw him on the other side of the road, sitting on a scooter and doing his hair in one of the many mirrors, it instantly took me back to the mid-sixties when he used to wait for me to finish my shift at work. He knew I'd remember so I played along with him.

"Alright Jim? What you doing?"

"I'm waiting for you. I thought I'd give yer a lift". He smiled and I laughed as I put my arms round him and gave him a peck on the cheek.

"Nah, sod off. I'm not getting on that; I've just had my hair done".

"Yeah, not the same when you've gotta put a crash hat on is it? Come on, jump up. Don't be so fucking boring".

"Nice to see you're getting your old charm back. Fine".

"I thought we'd get something to eat before we get to Judy's. She's a shit cook".

"Alright then, but not too far. I remember how uncomfortable these things are".

It only took us five minutes to get to the sea front where he parked up and we went down the steps by the pier to the same café we used to hang out at back in the sixties. It brought back a lot of memories. Not much had changed apart from a few kiddie's rides along the beach.

"So, Bunny… what brings you down 'ere"?

"I need to talk to Dave. It's over Jim. I've had enough".

"Oh dear. He ain't gonna take that too well. There's nothing like kicking a man when he's down".

"Yeah, and why's he down? It's nothing to do with me. It's all his own doing".

"To be fair, you enjoyed the proceeds of what Dave was up to as well".

"Yeah you're right, and if it was just about the money we would probably have worked through it, but shagging some little tart? No, that's it".

"I thought you two were into all that open marriage, shagging around stuff".

"We were a long time ago, but it was always more Dave than me. I just went along with it. Don't get me wrong, I enjoyed it, but I thought we knocked it all on the head. Dave obviously thought different though. I think I've just outgrown him. I want someone who loves and cares about me."

I could see Jimmy getting all gooey-eyed and hopeful, so before we went any further I thought I'd put him straight.

"And before you start building your hopes up, I've found someone".

"I never did stand a chance, did I"?

"I wouldn't say that, I did fancy yer or I wouldn't have shagged you would I"?

"It was over there by the pier".

"What was"?

"Where we had a shag".

"God! You can even remember the exact spot".

"So, who's the lucky fella then? Is it someone I know"?

"I'm not saying nothing until I've spoken to Dave first. What about you Jim? How you coping since Tracy died"?

"I'm not too bad now, but I still can't face going to the club".

"You loved that club and it's a good place to meet someone else when you're ready."

"I 'ave started to get really friendly with someone actually. She's a lovely girl".

"Do I know her"?

"You might do. Her name's Nadia, one of the girls at the agency, a blonde, Russian bird".

"Jim, don't be so fucking stupid".

"Hang on a minute. I said she's a lovely girl and I get on well with her, not that I was gonna marry her".

When Jim said about the Russian girl I started to panic. I know what Jim's like – he pours his heart out and tells people everything. It was too much of a coincidence that Russians were after them and while Jim was driving one around.

"You didn't tell her you were coming down here, did you"?

"No. Why"?

"No reason. You love it here in Brighton, don't yer"?

"It's always been a special place for me. In fact, I'm thinking of selling the club and moving down. I fancy opening a clothes shop and selling all the gear I like".

"What, a Mod shop"?

"Yeah".

"Is there much demand for that sort of thing then"?

"Yeah, it's still a big scene. You saw what it was like on the Isle of Wight".

"Yeah, it was crazy. You're like a load of big kids, still riding round on scooters".

"It's a laugh, Bunny. It's escapism. It feels good to be part of something that's fun, instead of all that shit that Dave and the others are into. Ron and Charlie are back into it as well. They were always up the club and they've both got scooters again. In fact, they're staying at Judy's as well".

"You're kidding".

"No, I'm not. You know what a prat Ron is: he took a contract on refitting night clubs, him and Charlie bought all the materials up front and the owners of the club went bust, so they're skint again".

"It wouldn't have had anything to do with Ray, would it"?

"Yeah, I think it was. How did you know"?

"There's a lot going on, Jim. We all need to talk, but first I need to sort things out with Dave".

Jimmy took me to Judy's, a big old town house, where I could hear the music from the end of the path. I walked in and there they all were: Rudy was over by the window puffing a huge joint, Ron and Charlie were playing pool, and Dave was crashed out in a chair with an empty bottle of Jack Daniels sitting on the table next to him. There was no sign of Judy or Roger though. Once I'd said my hellos I gave Dave a shake to wake him up. He got out the chair to give me a hug and he stunk. It weren't just the booze I could smell.

"Get off me. You're disgusting! Go and get cleaned up. You stink".

"Well that's nice, ain't it lads? I ain't seen my darling wife for ages and when I do, she pushes me away and tells me I stink".

"Dave you do stink. Go and get cleaned up". Jimmy stuck up for me, followed quickly by Rudy.

"Yeah, man and clean that tub up after you 'cos I'm getting ready next".

Rudy took a long hard draw on his joint, then puffed a huge cloud of smoke out the window. He put it out and came to sit next to me.

"You looking stunning as ever girl. You 'ave a glow about you, babe. Why you still with that man? You deserve better – I've been hearing bad things 'bout him babe".

"I know. That's why I'm here; I've had enough".

Just as I said it Judy walked in behind.

"Did I hear right? You've had enough of Dave"?

"Keep it down a bit. I ain't told him yet".

Charlie took a shot then said,

"I think he's figured that out already. That's why he's in such a state". I felt a pang of guilt at that, so I changed the attention to Judy.

"So Judy, how you keeping? You're looking good. I bet you'll be glad to see the back of this lot, won't you"?

"No. It's been a bit of a laugh remembering old times. I won't miss that Roger though. He's a right miserable git".

"Where is he"?

"He's out fishing. He's always out fishing".

Jimmy tried to cheer us all up and get the mood elevated with a little plan,

"Thought we'd all go out tonight. The ballroom's still there, you know".

"I thought they would have pulled that down by now". I was surprised.

"Nah, they done it up a few years back and I know the bloke who runs it. There's a great DJ called Wolfy and he's one of the faces.

He does a lot for the scene".

"Another one of your mates is he"?

"Yeah. He's really well connected; he's mates with *The Who* and that".

"Blimey".

"He's a bit of a nutter, but he just oozes Mod".

"Sounds good to me. I look forward to meeting him. I need a laugh, I need to have a chat with Dave first though, and we'll catch up with yer later".

Me and Judy carried on talking, Jimmy joined Ron and Charlie playing pool, and Rudy lit up another joint and chilled out by the window. Me and Judy went up to her bedroom to pick something to wear later. She had some really lovely clothes, but she decided to wear a short dog-toothed check skirt and jacket.

"What do you think"?

"If it was thirty years ago, I'd say you look great, but you've got loads of other stuff in here nicer than that".

"I know, but Jimmy still loves this sort of thing, don't he"?

"You still fancy him, don't yer"?

"Yeah I do, but he ain't noticed yet. I think he fancies someone back home, but I'm working on it".

"You've got nothing to worry about there. I know who he likes and I also know for a fact that it's not going anywhere. Oh my God, I remember now; you always fancied him when we all used to knock about".

"Yeah I did, but he always fancied you. I came close to getting off with him a few times at parties, then you'd walk in and he didn't want to know. When you ended up with Dave I thought I finally had my chance and the silly sod ends up going inside. I always kept in touch with him, but then I met Bob and moved to America".

"Do you regret going to America"?

"No. I had a great time and I did really love Bob, but I wish we had had kids. If we had, I think we would still be together now. Yeah, I'd say that was my biggest regret: not having kids. Still, it's too late now, so what you don't have, you don't miss".

I smiled at Judy and, not realising it, I had my hand on my belly as I replied.

"It's not too late, you know".

"Oh my God. You're pregnant".

"Yeah, I am".

"How do think Dave will take it"?

"Not very well 'cos it ain't his".

"Are you sure"?

"I'm sure alright. I've been screwing Dave for nearly twenty years without protection, so if Dave was gonna get me pregnant I think it would've happened by now. It's definitely my new fella's".

"What do you mean, no protection? I thought you didn't want kids".

"I didn't at first, but when I got to twenty-five I did. We had some terrible rows over it and, in the end, Dave agreed, so I came off the pill and we decided if it happened, it happened, but it never did. I thought there was something wrong with me, so it was easier to tell people we didn't want kids. Turns out it weren't me with the problem though, so it must have been Dave firing blanks".

"It definitely is over then"?

"Yeah, and when he's ready we'll go somewhere quiet and I'll tell him".

Me and Judy carried on talking so I didn't realise the time until she pointed out that Dave had been getting ready for well over a hour, so I went in his room to tell him to hurry up. I walked in his room and there was clothes and empty bottles of booze everywhere and Dave lying face down on his bed. I shook him.

"Get up! Get up"!

"Alright, alright. Calm down. I must have fell asleep".

"Passed out, more like. Come on, I've been waiting for you

to sort yourself out".

"Stick the kettle on and do us a black coffee, will you? By the time it's ready to drink, I'll be showered and shaved and ready to go".

I went downstairs, made the coffee and waited for Dave back in the main room with the others. Charlie and Ron were still playing pool, Rudy was completely stoned with headphones on listening to his Reggae, and Roger had got back and was talking to Jimmy. I said hello to Roger and he just looked up and nodded. He was too engrossed in conversation with Jimmy, so I just sat down and flicked through one of Judy's magazines. Dave emerged fifteen minutes later looking terrible. He had bits of tissue stuck to his face where he'd cut himself shaving, his hair needed a good cut, and the suit he had on was two sizes too small. Charlie burst out laughing, but Jimmy weren't impressed.

"Dave, get my fucking suit off".

"Leave it out, Jim. You've got loads up there".

"Get it off. I 'aven't even worn that yet and it set me back eight hundred quid".

"Well, you was done mate. I leaned down to do my shoes up and the seam split. It ain't made very well".

"It was made exceptionally well, which is why it set me back eight hundred, but it was made to fit me, not you, you fat fucker". Everyone saw the funny side of it with even Roger managing a smile, but poor Jimmy was distraught. He took great pride in his clothes. To make matters worse, Dave took a sip of his coffee and dripped some down the trousers.

"You dirty, fat, slob. Look what you've done! You've ruined it". Jimmy was practically crying.

"It'll wash out".

"No, it won't. That's top quality mohair, you prat".

"I'll get you another one when this mess is sorted out".

"I wouldn't be too sure about that".

"Sounds like you know something we don't", said Roger.

"Yeah love, what do yer know"?

"All I know is I ain't going nowhere with you looking like that. Go and get something on that at least fits".

He went back upstairs to get changed and I could tell by the way the others were talking about him that they had had enough. He came back down in jeans, trainers and a T-shirt, which was good because he wouldn't be getting in the Ballroom dressed like that. We went for a walk along the seafront and stopped at a bench that looked out to sea.

"It's all gone wrong, ain't it love"?

"Yeah, it has. You've really messed things up".

"We both have. You enjoyed living off that business as much as I did".

"Yeah I did, but I didn't screw a fifteen year old kid, did I"?

"Leave it out. How was I to know she was fifteen? You saw her".

"Yeah, I did and you're right, she looked all of eighteen, but the age isn't the point. You promised you wouldn't get off with the girls and I've since found out that you've screwed practically all of them".

"Yeah, there's no point denying it; I have. I couldn't resist it. It's like putting a kid in charge of a sweet shop and telling them they can't 'ave any, but you know it didn't mean anything. It was just sex".

"Listen to yourself. You never once stopped to think how shagging a girl thirty years younger than me would make me feel".

"No, I didn't, but to be fair love, I didn't think you'd find out".

"Well, I did and that's it. We're finished."

"Don't be like that. We can work through this. It's just another chapter in our crazy lives".

"No, Dave. It's the final chapter, the end".

"You're serious, ain't yer"?

"Yeah, I am. In fact, I've met someone else already".

"Fuck me. You didn't waste no time, did yer? Who is he"?

"You don't need to know. All you need to know is this is the happiest I've ever been".

"Hang on a minute. In the space of a few months you've lost everything: the house, the business, and me, who you've been with nearly thirty years, and you're blissfully happy? What's so fucking wonderful about this new bloke then"?

"We love each other and it feels great".

"We loved each other".

"Did we? I don't think we really did. We had a laugh and we cared about each other, but it wasn't love. I know that now because he makes me feel like you never did".

Dave was gutted. I could see tears starting to well up in his eyes as we sat and talked about all the good times we'd had. I could tell he was trying to talk me round and he wasn't going to give up, so I thought I'd tell him that I was pregnant. Then he'd know there was definitely no more "us".

"I can see what you're trying to do Dave, but I've definitely made my mind up".

"After all them good times we had, you're telling me it's over? Well I don't believe you and I won't accept it".He was starting to get a bit angry, which was unlike Dave. It must have been the whisky talking, so I didn't prolong it any further.

"I'm pregnant".

"Pregnant? You're fucking joking".

"No, I'm not".

"Well it definitely ain't mine".

"Why you so sure"?

"'Cos I had the snip years ago".

"You did what"? He sat there laughing while I descended into a state of shock. I couldn't believe what he'd just said, but most of all, how flippant he was.

"When did you have it? How many years ago"?

"I don't know. It was when you kept banging on about wanting a kid. You knew I didn't want a fucking kid, so when I went to the States for that three week fishing trip, I had it done then".

"You bastard. All these years you've made me feel like there was something wrong with me. Why weren't you honest with me when I was young enough? I could have met someone who did want kids".

"Yeah, course you would and where would that have left me"?

"You would have met someone else".

"Yeah, I would, and eventually they would have wanted kids too. What's the matter with you fucking women? Why do you all want poxy kids"?

I was speechless as I got up to walk away and he sneered,

"Yeah, go on, fuck off. I wouldn't want yer now you're knocked up anyway".

I walked back to Judy's tears streaming out my eyes and head thumping. By the time I got back, I'd managed to pull myself together, but I went straight up to my room 'cos I couldn't face anyone. Judy followed and asked me how I got on. I couldn't talk. I needed time to get my head round what Dave had said. In the space of a couple of hours, I'd gone from pitying him to feeling sorry for him and actually thinking that I still cared for him, to hating him. I know I shouldn't have done, but I had to have a stiff drink to calm myself down. As they were leaving to go up the club, Jimmy shouted up to me,

"Bunny, you coming"?

"No, I don't feel too good".

"Well at least come down and 'ave a butcher's at me. I look

fucking handsome. Come and 'ave a look at this suit – it's the nuts".

I went down to see them off and Jim was right; he looked great and so did Judy. They looked like they'd stepped back in time thirty years.

"You and Judy make a great couple".

"Yeah, we do. Judy scrubs up alright don't she? Talking of couples, where's Dave? He didn't come back. Did you 'ave a barney"?

"Yeah, we did. I left him near the beach".

"He'll probably turn up later. We're off".

"Have a great time".

They all left and I just cried myself to sleep. I got up at ten on Saturday morning and went down to the dining room where everyone was up and eating their breakfast. The radio was on and they were all talking about what a great night it had been. Jimmy greeted me with a grin.

"Morning gorgeous. You missed a great night. You would have loved it! At about twelve, Wolfy was playing all the old Motown and sixties stuff. "Sounds great. Did Dave go"?

"No, I ain't seen him this morning. The lazy git's still in bed".

"He's not in bed, man. I just been in his room to get my cassette player". Rudy disagreed.

"You must have had a right ding dong yesterday. He didn't come back".

"What was the row about then"? asked Ron.

"It wasn't a row. I just told him it's over".

"Nice. You finally blew him out". Rudy was pleased at least. Charlie interjected with his gem of wisdom,

"Knowing Dave, he probably pulled some bird to cheer himself up".

It was eleven o'clock when the news came on the radio.

"Police are appealing to anyone who might be able to identify a white male in his mid to late forties who was found at Beachy Head earlier today. Circumstances suggest suicide".

Roger was first to break the silence that followed.

"It looks like he didn't take it too well, you blowing him out, love".

"We don't know it's definitely Dave do we"? Jimmy tried to kindle some hope.

"It's Dave alright. He said years ago that he couldn't live without me".

"One of us is going to have to make sure", whispered Judy.

"I will", Charlie volunteered, "Jim can I take your scooter"?

"Yeah take it. Let us know straight away".

I couldn't take it in. I was still in shock from what he'd said to me the day before. I could hear everyone's voices around me, but nothing was registering in my head so I went up to my room. I sat on the chair by the window where I could see the bench we'd sat on and talked for so long. I could picture him sitting there, smiling and laughing as we reminisced about the numerous good times we had. I sat there just staring into space until Judy and Jimmy came into the room. Charlie had just called to confirm it was Dave. Jimmy couldn't get his head round it and Judy was wiping the tears from her eyes. They wanted answers, so I told them exactly what Dave had said and Jimmy just sat there, shaking his head from side to side as he said,

"Nah, that's bollocks. Dave never had the snip. He didn't have to 'cos he couldn't have kids. I don't know quite what was wrong with him, but he had some kind of operation when he was a kid. It was something to do with his prostate".

"He told me he went to America and had it done there".

"He went to America to have an op to try and put him right. He knew how much you wanted kids and it gutted him he couldn't give you any".

"Why didn't he tell me"?

"He didn't tell yer 'cos he was shit scared of losing yer".

Now I knew the reason for all them rows we had years ago about kids, I started to feel really guilty.

"I feel terrible. He's killed himself because I'm pregnant and I finished with him".

Judy put her arms round me to give me a comforting hug and said,

"No, he didn't. It's not your fault. Dave was messed up and we all knew that".

"I don't mean to make you feel bad Bunny, but yeah. You're right".

Before Jimmy could continue Judy gave him a dagger look.

"Jimmy"!

"Well he did! But yeah, Judy, you're right. He was messed up. The trouble with Dave was he was a selfish bastard. If he wanted something he got it. He'd shag someone's wife or girlfriend and not give a shit about the consequences. He's always been the same and that's why he topped himself. I bet he never once thought of us lot. The fact that I've just lost my wife and now I've gotta deal with losing my best mate never crossed his mind. And look at the state of you; you're pregnant, which should be the happiest time of your life. No, don't feel guilty. What was you supposed to do? Stay with him for the rest of your life being unhappy and miserable just so he didn't top himself? All the time he'd have been putting it about and 'aving a great time".

"Jim's right".

"I know he is. Just leave me for a minute".

"Come on Jim. You as well".

They went downstairs and left me to get my head round what had happened. Jimmy was right about me leaving Dave and being pregnant pushing Dave over the edge, but seeing the state of him, there was a good chance he would have done it anyway. There's no way he could have done a long prison sentence. I sat and reminisced about the good times when it was just me and Dave, while judging by the noise of laughter from downstairs, they were remembering the crazy times. It was great hearing them laughing and talking so I just sat and listened to them for ages. I could hear Jimmy's voice the loudest.

"Yeah we had some great times and most of them were in the sixties when we were Mods".

"What you on about? You spent most of the sixties behind bars", said Ron, "You missed the best part from sixty-five to sixty-nine. That's why you're so into it now".

"So are you and Charlie".

"Not like you, we're not. Alright, it's a bit of a laugh going on some of the rallies with yer and the occasional sunny Sunday ride out on the scooters is good, but you live and breathe Mod. We don't. I mean look at Charlie sitting there in his flip flops and cut down jeans. You wouldn't be seen dead in that".

"No, you're right. He's a fucking state".

"I'm comfortable, Jim, which is more than I can say for you sitting there in them bollock-crushing Levi's".

"You're right though; I did miss out. How do you think I felt banged up inside with a load of psychos, murderers, rapists and gangsters while you lot were out 'aving a laugh? Not one of you fuckers bothered to come and see me".

"I did", said Judy.

"Fuck off, Jim. You were in Strangeways, which weren't exactly round the corner, was it? Besides, you were fucking nuts back then", protested Ron. Jimmy was focussed on what Judy had said though.

"Yeah you did, didn't yer Judy? In fact, you've always been there for me".

"Get the fucking violins out. Poor Jimmy's had a rough time.

If it weren't for you getting banged up and mixing with all those psychos and gangsters you talk so dismissively about, you wouldn't have had what you've got now", Roger was being a sarky bastard as usual.

"Yeah, well things ain't that rosy".

Rudy tried to put a positive spin on it,

"Tings aren't so down for you, man. You got a lot more than we. Losing that sweet girl of yours is 'eavy shit to have to deal with, but you still have the club".

"'Ere Rudy", asked Ron, "what's with all the Jamaican lingo? I always remember you talking like us".

"That's 'cos I spent a lot of time round you geezers and when I got back home and started mixing with my brothers again I got back to my roots".

"So why come back here if you was getting back to your roots"? Roger again.

"Because someone back here got a big mouth".

"Who's that then"?

"It's a long story man. It all began…"

"'Ang on. Roger, trust me, it's a fucking long story. Let's just say he got fucked".

"Yeah, man. I got fucked."

"Fuck me. None of us is having much luck are we? You've lost Tracy, Rudy's had to come out of retirement, Roger's on the run, me and Ron got fucked over and, to top it all, Dave gets set up and ends up topping himself. What next"? Charlie wanted to know.

"I don't know, but we'll soon find out. I just got a call from Ken. He's at the station with young Steve, he wants picking up, and he sounds well worried".

"I'll get 'em", volunteered Judy.

"So Charlie, what happened to you two clowns then? I thought you were in the building game", said Roger.

"We were and we was doing alright until we started working

for that flash cunt, Ray".

"Go on".

"We done a big refit on one of his clubs in Southend".

"Yeah, it was a good little number. We worked all day and were on the piss all night and he put us up in this posh hotel".

"Yeah we thought he was loaded. We were buying the materials up front and at the end of the week he weighed us out. We done alright, but then he got us to do a refit on a casino and the gear we were putting in there cost a fortune.

"It was the same crack as the other club", Ron took over the story. "We bought all the materials and he weighed us out at the end of the week. Trouble is, he fucked off on holiday for three weeks and no-one from his company was authorised to get cash out".

"We had enough dough to get all the gear, but it was tight. Anyway he comes back, brown as a fucking berry, and tells us his company went bankrupt. Apparently the only way we can get our dough is to try getting it from the company that bought the assets".

"What company was that"? asked Roger.

"Something Holdings Ltd", supplied Ron.

"DW Holdings", said Roger.

"Yeah that was them. Bastards more or less told us to fuck off and we lost nearly a hundred grand".

"How did you know who they were, Roger"? Jimmy asked. "I don't know what the fuck's going on, but they fucked me over as well".

Judy must have come back with Steve and Ken at that point because Jimmy said,

"Alright Ken? Alright Steve? How you doing? It's good to be back in Brighton, ain't it"

"Yeah. I would've come down on the scooter, but Vinny told us to get down a bit sharpish".

"Vinny did? Why's that then"? asked Roger.

"Dunno. He said he'd explain later".

"What the fuck is going on and what's Vinny got to do with it all"? Jimmy wanted to know.

"I don't see much of him", said Roger.

"Nah, nor do I. The last time I saw him he was off to see his sister, Doreen".

"Doreen's his sister"? Ken sounded shit scared.

"How do you know Doreen?"

"I don't. I just didn't know he had a sister, that's all".

"I've got a horrible feeling Vinny's up to something with Doreen".

"I hope not 'cos the last time I heard from Helen she was going down the hospital with Vinny to see her Dad. Apparently he was in a crash".

"Jack's been involved in a crash? Is he alright"?

"I don't know I've been trying to ring her, but she ain't answering".

"It all makes fucking sense now, don't it"? Said Jimmy.

"What does"?

"What 'ave we all got in common? Don't try and work that out, Ron 'cos we'll be 'ere all week. I'll tell yer – all of us, in some way, fucked Mike up, didn't we? That bitch Doreen's behind all this and it looks like Vinny's helping her".

"We don't know that", said Roger. I was glad he was defending Vinny.

"Leave it out. It don't take a genius to work it out. Who's the only one who's doing alright"? argued Jimmy.

"Vinny". answered Judy immediately. "Oh my God! He not only took Dave's agency, but I bet he's Bunny's new fella".

"What about you Jim"? countered Roger. "You're doing alright. You've still got your club and shop, so you ain't lost fuck all".

"Perhaps she ain't got round to me yet".

I'd sat in the bedroom and heard enough. It was time to fill them in, so I marched in and told him quickly to get it over with.

"She has Jim, and you've lost more than anyone".

"What do you mean, Bunny"?

"She killed Tracy. Doreen killed Tracy".

"She killed Tracy? No, it was a drunk driver. It was an accident". He couldn't take it in.

"The only accident was she killed Tracy and not you. It was you she wanted dead".Poor Jimmy looked like he was going to pass out. the colour drained from his face as he poured himself another drink.

"Fucking ''ell. We need to get on to the Old Bill", said Ron.

"What about that copper that helped last time? That one that Jack knew"? asked Charlie.

"Don't you read the papers or watch the news"? Roger sneered. "He was found bobbing about in the Thames last week".

"Yeah, I read something about that. I didn't realise it was him", said Charlie. Roger was keen to fill him in.

"My mate knows a copper and apparently he was shot in the kneecaps and shoulders first, then thrown in the Thames to drown just before he bled to death. Whoever done it was one sick twisted fucker".

"And Judy, you're right. Me and Vinny are a couple".

"Vinny? What the fuck do you see in him"? Jimmy was obviously still jealous.

"I see a side of him that none of you see. We're very close and before any of you judge him, I'd hold fire until you've heard what he's got to say. He could be the one person who can get you all out of this".

To say it was a tense Saturday afternoon and night was an understatement. Everyone was scared, especially when Roger told them the gory details about Charles the copper.

Me and Judy went out for dinner, Roger went fishing, Rudy stayed in sitting on the balcony getting stoned and listening to his Reggae, while the others all went out and got pissed. Everyone got up surprisingly early Sunday morning 'cos I don't think anyone slept well. Vinny arrived at twelve and Jimmy welcomed him in.

"Come in, Vinny. Fill us all in. We're dying to know what's going on".

"It's a right fucking mess. I've just about got my head round it, but before I start get yourselves a drink and make yourselves comfortable".

We all dispersed and clattered around pouring drinks and arranging ourselves so we could all listen to Vinny. When we were settled, Charlie said,

"Go on".

"Where's Dave"? asked Vinny. "We'd better wait for him".

"I haven't had a chance to tell you. He's dead"?

"Dead"?

"As a fucking dodo, chimed in Roger, helpfully. "Straight off Beachy Head".

"Fucking idiot".

"A very unhappy idiot" Supplied Judy.

"I guess finding out Bunny was up the duff was the final straw" Said Jimmy.

"Jim"! exclaimed Judy, for the second time in two days.

"Sorry. Weren't you supposed to know".

"Fuck me. Is there anything else you ain't had a chance to tell me? I think we need a little chat first".

"Congratulations and all that, but I think there's more important things we need to talk about than your poxy baby plans". Roger was getting impatient.

"Yeah, man. We need to know what's happening", said Rudy.

"I don't know what she's done to you, Charlie and Rudy, but her plans don't include you".

"Hasn't she done enough to me? She killed Tracy".

"I know mate, and trust me she ain't finished yet. I don't know where to start".

"Try starting with that day I popped round to yours and you was off to see her", suggested Jimmy.

"Yeah, that was the start of it actually. She told me that you was all taking the piss out of me. She reckoned that after we got back from the Isle of Wight, Rudy done a little detour with that coke and Dave, Roger, Jack and you were making a fortune selling it".

"What? I never make no detour. I take it straight to Dave's old place in Kent", protested Rudy.

"You seriously believed that? Knowing how shit scared I was of getting banged up again"?

"I didn't at first, but then she showed me a statement for a foreign bank account with your names on it. There was fucking millions in there".

"Jesus, Vinny. You know I didn't touch drugs", said Jimmy.

"I know you don't. She reckoned that your part in it all was using the bike shop to get the gear in the country".

When Vinny said that the colour drained from Ken's face and he put his head in his hands.

"Shall I tell him Ken? Or do you wanna do the honours"? Vinny asked.

"Tell me what? Ken what the fuck 'ave you been up to"?

"I didn't know, honest".

"Know what? What the fuck's going on"?

Ken opened his mouth, but Vinny interrupted him.

"'Ang on a minute Ken. We'll get to that in a minute. Anyway, she reckoned that Dave knew a Russian hooker who helped him set up a deal in India".

"It weren't Dave. It was Ray who knew the Russian hooker" Said Roger.

"I know that now".

"Yeah I know a Russian hooker", grinned Jimmy, like an idiot.

"It ain't Nadia Jim. It's the other one", said Vinny. Steve had been moving his head back and forth like a tennis umpire up to this point, but he had clearly had enough.

"You all lost me. I'm getting out of here as this is obviously nothing to do with me".

"Sit down Steve". Vinny was firm and it stopped Steve in his tracks. "It's got everything to do with you, thanks to your Dad because it was your Dad and Jim who was bringing in fucking millions worth of heroin in from India in crates of old scooters. We'll get to that in a minute though. The reason I started up my agency was that Doreen had told me enough to convince me something was going on. That's why I went to see you, Jim, after my meeting with her. Then, when you told me that you was stashing as much cash as possible so you and Tracy could fuck off to Portugal, I was beginning to think what she said was true".

"Fucking 'ell Vinny. When I said I was stashing cash, I meant five or six hundred a month, not fucking five or six million".

"Well, I didn't know that, did I? She showed me a statement with eight fucking million in".

"I don't believe this". He was sitting there with his mouth hanging open, looking like he'd been winded.

"Anyway", continued Vinny, "I was well pissed off, so when she offered to help me set up a rival agency to Dave's, I thought fuck it. I will. I didn't realise she was gonna set Dave up like that".

"She's Mike's daughter alright. Clever bitch". Roger had recovered a bit now and was getting to the anger stage.

"It gets worse, trust me. Dave got shut down and I nick all his girls and punters".

"And his fucking missus, you nasty cunt".

"It weren't like that, Jim", I said. Vinny didn't know we would fall in love, so I couldn't have them all thinking he'd planned it that way.

"Weren't it? Well that's what it looks like to me".

"The only reason I got Bunny to work for me is that I couldn't cope and she knew the business inside out".

"Fuck me", said Ken, "It didn't take you long to get over Dave".

"Ken, with all due respect, you know nothing about me and Dave. We were as good as over way before all this and him getting off with that kid was the final straw whether he was set up or not. Who are you to judge me anyway? You're half the reason we're all in this mess".

"Yeah, shut the fuck up Ken. I'll get to you in a minute. Anyway me and Bunny started getting really close and I told her more or less the full story".

"What haven't you told me? What's going on"? I didn't want no more lies.

"'Ang on a minute. Before we go any further, I wanna know what you've been up to Ken", Jimmy was fuming.

"Yeah, Dad", said Steven.

"Shall I tell 'em"? asked Vinny again.

"No, I will". He took a deep breath. "Well, I got in the shit again with big Steve, the money lender".

"Fucking ''ell. He ain't involved as well is he"? Jim asked.

"Nah, listen and I'll fucking tell yer. I owed him ten grand".

"Dad, you said you wouldn't gamble again".

"I've always gambled. When I got in the shit last time, your mum accepted I weren't gonna change, so she thought she could control it by giving me an allowance each week. I felt like a little kid getting fucking pocket money. It was humiliating".

"Little kid? You're worse than a little kid; you're pathetic". Jimmy was really laying into him.

"Anyway, I started skimming money from the shop. Not a lot, just a few quid here and there when I done cash jobs. Then you came and worked there and that put paid to that, so that's when

I started borrowing off big Steve again. He used to be a bit tasty, but he was getting on a bit so I weren't too worried, but he sold my debt on".

"And don't tell me; Doreen bought it"? Roger was catching onto this game.

"Yeah, that's right and the bitch was adding ten per cent interest each month, which I couldn't pay. Anyway I was walking home from the pub, half pissed, and her two 'eavys shove me in a van and there's this other geezer in there called Andy and he was telling me how his debt got right out of control".

"So you let her smuggle drugs into the country through the shop in return for her writing off your poxy ten grand"? Roger asked.

"You fucking idiot. Why didn't you just come to me"? said Jim.

"It weren't like that".

"Well how was it then, Dad"?

"They took us to this warehouse and asked Andy if he was gonna pay up. When he said he couldn't she told him he was no use to her and this little creepy geezer blew his fucking brains out. There was fucking claret everywhere and I was shitting myself. I told her I didn't 'ave the money, but she said it didn't matter 'cos she'd write it off as long as I changed the contacts in India and started using a different shipping company. When the containers came in we picked the scooters up and that was that".

"And that's all"? asked Jim, his voice dangerously quiet now. Ken wriggled, sweat glistening on his forehead.

"No. The bonus was we didn't 'ave to pay for the shipment. The geezer from India faxed over the invoice and you had to sign it, Jim".

"I never signed no invoices".

"No, I did it for yer".

"But fifteen grand used to come out the bike shop's account", said Steve, who was still confused.

"Yeah and you were drawing it out, Ken, and using it to fucking gamble. You fucking idiot. You've put me right in the frame".

"How was I to know they were smuggling drugs in"?

"Well it wouldn't have been fucking popadoms, would it? You prat"! Roger exploded.

"Shut up Roger", said Jimmy. "Fucking ''ell. She's setting me up with the Old Bill. Jesus, I'll do fifteen years for that". "You've all been set up alright", Vinny continued, "but it's not the Old Bill. It's worse than that".

"Fucking worse? What's worse"?

"Clever cow. The Russians". Roger had worked it all out now.

"Russians? What the fuck 'ave Russians got to do with it"? Jimmy was beside himself, but Vinny carried on regardless.

Yeah Russians. You see, Ray had a taste for foreign hookers and he starts seeing this bird called Nadine. Well Nadine is over here because she set up some nasty bastard Russian gangster and he's now doing hard time in fucking Siberia. You see, the Russians love a bit of brown".

"Brown? What's brown"? Steve wanted to know.

"Heroin. Yeah, the Russians love to chase the dragon and they had the heroin trade from Afghanistan well sown up for years. Virtually all heroin coming into this country had its origins in Russia. This Nadine bird knew all the right contacts to get the shit, but not the means to get it over here".

"And that's where you came in, Ken", said Roger.

"I didn't know all this did I"?

"No. Doreen buying your debt was a real fluke. She was gonna make you sweat for a while, then you would have ended up the same as that geezer, Andy. When she told Ray all about you, that's when they come up with their plan to get it in the country. It was a perfect set up: they get the heroin and you all take the blame".

"So, we've now got a load of pissed off Russians after us". Jimmy summed it up nicely.

"Oh yes, and trust me – they are well pissed off. Not only do they think you've cost them millions in lost trade, but they think you've all been working with Nadine. To top it off, the bloke who's running the show is Boris and it's his twin brother doing hard time in fucking Siberia".

"You've gotta take your hat off to her. It's a stroke of pure genius". said Roger.

"Yeah, fucking great. Let's give her a pat on the back and a fucking Blue Peter badge. What the fuck are we gonna do"? asked Ken.

"I ain't finished yet; it gets a whole lot messier. You lot were small fry. She's made a lot of money through this little scam with the Russians, but now she's going for the big one: she wants what Jack's got".

"Well she's pissing in the wind with that one. Jack's far too clever to be caught up in all this bollocks", Roger was pleased with that until I shot him down.

"Yeah, you're right. That's why she's taken Helen".

"How do you know"? asked Steve, panicked.

"Because I delivered her".

"Jack is gonna rain down a ton of shit on you son", cackled Roger. "I think I'd rather deal with the Russians".

"Vinny, why would you do that? She trusted you and so did Jack". Steve was upset and he was trying to make sense of it all.

"And why do you think that was, Vinny? Didn't you ever wonder why Jack and Mike hated each other"? asked Jim.

"I just put it down to Jack feeling sorry for me".

"No mate he didn't feel sorry for you. He loved yer because he's your Dad. You've handed your sister to Doreen on a plate".

"That's bollocks", laughed Vinny nervously. "What you going on about"?

"He let it slip a long time ago while we were in the nick".

"It explains why Mike hated you so much", Roger offered.

"Think about it: it's bad enough his missus dies giving birth to you, but if he finds out later his brother was knocking her off"

"I bet Doreen knows", said Vinny.

"You're being set up", Ken stated the obvious.

"Yeah, course I am. Why do you think I'm here? They've used me to get the agency set up so Ray can 'ave it when they've decided what to do with me".

"Does Jack know yet – that they've got the most precious thing in his life"? asked Roger.

"I don't know. The plan was to do the exchange on Wednesday", Vinny replied.

"And what is the exchange"?

"She wants Jack to sign over half of his estate".

"Fucking hell! That's millions".

"She reckoned about fifty million. Alex has done all the paperwork and he has it all ready to sign at the unit where they're holding her".

"Right, the first thing I've got to do is pay Jack a visit and let him know what's been going on. You lot just stay here and do nothing". Roger was taking charge of the situation, which felt good 'cos I'd been getting really worried about Vinny under all that stress.

When Roger had left to go and speak to Jack, I looked across at Ken and, although he was my brother-in-law, I wanted to kill him. "You fucking idiot, Ken. Look at the shit you've got us into".

"Leave it out Jim", Steve jumped to his defence, "you heard Roger; she was gonna get us all one way or another".

Steve was right. If Trace hadn't taken my scooter that night, I wouldn't even be here. I needed a break from the others, so I went for a ride on my scooter and ended up at Beachy Head, the spot where Dave had topped himself only the day before. You couldn't have picked a more peaceful, beautiful location; the sea looked so blue from up on the cliff and you could see the whole of Eastbourne from up here. I looked over the edge of the cliff and it seemed to pull me down. For a split second I even contemplated jumping and putting an end to this whole fucking nightmare, but now I knew Tracy's death wasn't an accident I wanted to see Doreen suffer. And I wanted to be the one to make it happen. I sat at the top of that cliff for over an hour, racking my brain thinking of ways to get out of this shit before it came to me.. I rushed back to tell the others. Bunny and Vinny were waiting for me when I got there.

"I've got a good idea".

"Go on", said Vinny.

"If we can tell the Russians what Doreen's been up to, then they'll sort her out for us".

"Me and Vinny have already thought of that", Bunny pissed on my plan immediately.

"Look mate, all them Russians are interested in is getting that Nadine bird and cutting out the competition", explained Vinny.

"And even if they were prepared to listen, how would you contact them"? asked Bunny, fucking negative again.

"That other Russian bird that I used to drive around – she might know. I got on really well with her and she had some Russian diplomats that used to book her".

"She might, but Roger's told us to stay here until he's spoken to Jack. If anyone can sort this mess out it's him", said Vinny.

"And what if he can't? Fuck it. I'm going to see Nadia to see if she can put us in touch with someone. She used to ask me enough questions, so now I'm gonna ask her a few".

"What do you mean 'ask enough questions'"? Vinny wanted to know.

"I told yer, didn't I? That day you was going to see Doreen".

"That's right – you did".

"I reckon she's got something to do with it. Why would she work for an escort agency and bring all her own clients"? Asked

Bunny.

"Yeah thinking about it, it don't make sense. Give her a bell Jim and find out".

"I ain't got her number, but I know where she was staying".

"Well what you waiting for? Go and see her", said Bunny.

"If you're gonna do it, you'd better be quick because as soon as Roger tells Jack he's gonna be down 'ere".

I borrowed Judy's car and went to the guest house she was staying at, but she'd checked out on the Friday. It was a bit of a long shot, but I went to the address I always took her on a Friday night; it was a big house in St Johns Wood. I sat outside for about half an hour. I could see two men inside and I was concentrating so much on what was going on inside the house that I didn't notice the car pull up behind me. There was a tap on my window and as I turned round there was Nadia by the side of the car with two geezers in suits. One of them opened my door and the other pulled me out. They took me inside the house and Nadia was talking to them in Russian all the while. She paused for a moment so I took the opportunity to interrupt.

"Nadia what's going on"?

"You tell me, Jim. Why you here"?

"I was looking for you".

"You find me. Now what do you want"? She was totally different to when I drove her around. She was cold and hard and she certainly weren't a hooker. I told her the whole story. The blokes there didn't understand a word I was saying, so they just sat around drinking Vodka. When I'd finished, she spoke to them for about fifteen minutes. She knew they wouldn't be interested in my long-winded story, only what was in it for them. Vinny was right – they didn't give a shit who they took out as long as their trade got back to normal. Nadia reckoned that we had cost them at least five million, so I offered them double back if they helped us out with Doreen. I figured if Jack got his daughter back for ten million, then it was better than the fifty that Doreen wanted. They let me go and gave me till Monday night to let them know. I rushed back down to Brighton, but it was gone midnight by the time I walked in. Jack was sitting there with two of his heavies and the rest looked very subdued.

"Hello Jim. Where have you been"? asked Jack.

"Yeah where have you been"? echoed Roger. "I told you to stay here and do fuck all, didn't I"?

"As it ''appens I might have solved our little problem".

"Little problem? I wouldn't say that. I'd say it was a fucking massive problem. They have my daughter, you cunt. It's a fucking mess".

I couldn't make Jack out, he was very hard to read and he was a sarcastic fucker, always making me feel on edge, but on this occasion I didn't feel at all nervous. Probably because I'd just spent a couple of hours not knowing whether I was gonna get a bullet in the back of my head or not.

"How did you get on, then"? asked Ken.

"Yeah go on. Let us all in", said Vinny.

"Well, I went to where she'd been staying, but she weren't there, so I went to that big house in St John's Wood where I always used to take her. I was sitting outside, watching the house, when there was a tap on my window and the next thing I knew these two big geezers in suits pulled me out the fucking car and Nadia asked me what I was doing".

"I bet you shit yourself", giggled Steve.

"So, she's in with the Russians then"? asked Bunny.

"Yeah, She's in with 'em alright".

"Can someone do me the honour of letting me know what the fuck's going on"? said Jack.

"I thought Roger explained it all", said Vinny.

"Listen son, the only thing I know is my Helen is being held by that psycho bitch and you handed her over on a silver fucking platter".

"Yeah that's right, Dad. I did".

"Dad? Fucking Dad"?

"I told him Jack", I said.

"Obviously, Jim. Doreen wouldn't have done it; she'd save that for when she blew your brains out".

"You reckon she would"? Vinny was incredulous.

"Yep. Without hesitation".

"So, why didn't you tell me you're my Dad"?

"I had my reasons, but now's not the time to discuss it. I'm more interested in what a load of Russians have got to do with me".

"They've got fuck all to do with you", said Roger. "Basically Doreen's been bringing in shit loads of heroin into the country via Jim's bike shop and she's set me, Ken, Steve and Jim up with a particularly nasty bunch of Russians".

"So if Nadia's in with the Russians why are you still 'ere then? Why did they let you go"? Vinny couldn't believe I'd got out of it alive.

"Well, I told her the whole story, didn't I? I went right back and she believed me and she wants to help, but you were right about her fucking comrades. They didn't give a shit. She reckons that Doreen's cost them about five million in lost trade. It didn't look good and I didn't think I was gonna get out of there, so I told them I could get what they lost back and another five million on top of that". Jack pissed himself laughing at that.

"Where are you gonna get ten mill from"?

"You". He stopped laughing.

"You are funny Jim. Ain't he funny, lads"?

"Well, I didn't think that was bad considering Doreen wants fifty for Helen".

"Do you honestly think I'm going to part with half of my estate and give it to that psycho bitch"?

"That's what she wants ain't it"? Surely he weren't gonna let something happen to Helen, just so he could keep his money.

"What she wants and what she gets are two different matters and I can tell you that she ain't getting fuck all. I've come down here to sort this mess out with Vinny: he knows where Helen is and he's going to help me get her back. Ain't that right, son"?

"Yeah that's right".

Jack was right. He didn't need to part with half his estate. He didn't even need to spend a penny to get Helen back. He did need Vinny's help though, so I followed him out to the kitchen, where he was making himself a sarnie.

"Vinny you've gotta help us out. If we don't give the Russians what they want, then it's fucking curtains for us. We're fucked without Jack's help".

"You heard him. He ain't parting with fuck all."

"Tell him you ain't gonna help get Helen back unless he helps us".

"I can't do that. She's my fucking sister".

"And we're your fucking mates".

"You are, but I don't give a fuck about Roger, and as for Ken, that fat useless fucker deserves it".

"And what about Steven? He don't deserve none of it".

"Yeah, I suppose you're right and, seeing the way he was with Helen that night, she'd be gutted if anything happened to him".

"That's right. Helen and Steve are together and Helen means the world to Jack. How would she feel if anything 'appened to Steve and her dad could have prevented it"?

"I'll give it a go, Jim".

We walked back into the lounge with our sarnies and a speck of hope. Vinny cleared his throat. You could tell he was nervous.

"Jack, you know Doreen's never going to give up. As soon as she finds out you've got one over on her, you'll always be looking over your shoulder. You'll have to take her, Ray, and the whole firm out if you're ever gonna sleep at night".

"You've got a point there, son".

"And how would you feel about Helen going out with Steven, knowing at any time some nutty fucking Russian could take him out? How bad are you gonna feel if Helen wants fuck all to do with you when she finds out you could have saved him"?

Jack didn't reply, he just got up, poured himself another drink and went over to the balcony where Rudy was sitting smoking his joint.

"Fuck me. There's Bob Marley out here".

"My name's Rudy".

"Well come in, Rudy, and join the fucking party".Rudy came in and they both sat down.

"So let me get this straight", Jack said. "These Russians want ten million and, in return, they take out Doreen and Ray".

"Yeah, that's it", I said, thinking he was coming round to the idea, before he said,

"I'm not happy about this. I know fuck all about Russians and I'm not happy about parting with ten million quid. How do we know if we can trust them? They might just take the money and run". My heart sank.

"Well, I thought once you get Helen out, they go in and we give 'em the money after".

"Wait a minute... Doreen's got a fucking fortune stashed away, so if we could find a way of getting hold of that we could use it to pay the Russians off".Vinny's turn for a great idea.

"And how you gonna do that"? asked Ken.

"I don't know, but I know a man who can".

"Who's that then, son"? Jack was interested.

"Alex, the accountant".

"Alex is still about? Well, fuck me. I thought he disappeared years ago. Now that is one clever man".

"What if we can get to him and make it worth his while"?

Asked Roger.

"Sure. There's no loyalty with Alex; he offers his services to the highest bidder", said Jack.

It was about four in the morning when Roger and Vinny set off for Alex's place. We all went to bed to try and get some kip and I don't know about the others, but I didn't sleep a wink. Everyone was up by nine and Roger and Vinny were back with Alex at ten. When he walked in he went straight up to Jack and shook his hand.

"Alright Jack? How you keeping? business good, is it"?

"Couldn't be better", Jack replied.

"You know I've got nothing to do with all this, don't you"?

"Yeah. As usual, you're just doing the books".

"That's right and keeping the books for Doreen is a fucking challenge, to say the least".

"Roger and Vinny have filled you in have they"?

"Yeah they have".

"What do you reckon"?

"You know me – it's doable. I can get five mill in cash, but what I want is the rest. I want her apartment and I want all Ray's clubs".

Jack and Alex went into the dining room to go over all the fine details. When they emerged an hour later, Alex went straight back home and Jack came over to the pool table where I was playing Roger. He was cool and collected. He didn't come across as a Dad whose daughter was in the hands of a psycho.

"I'll play the winner", he said.

"Shouldn't take me long", I replied.

"It's not over yet, Jim", said Roger, indignantly.

"It soon will be. In case you hadn't noticed, there's six stripes still up and only one spot". Roger smiled, leaned back, chalked his cue and then proceeded to clear the fucking table.

"And there you have it; the difference between cocky and confident. Jack laughed. "You've always been a cocky little fucker Jim. It's not a bad thing; it's all part of your charm, but it's also why you get yourself in the shit all the time".

"'Ang on a minute. This mess ain't all down to me". "I suppose you've all been fucking stupid, actually. Especially you, son". He addressed Vinny.

"Doreen's very clever".

"She's clever alright. Alex has been filling me in. She's been plotting this for nearly three years. She's one very bitter and dangerous woman; she's inherited Mike's psychotic tendencies and her mother's intelligence – a lethal combination. You thought Mike was bad, well he was, but he weren't the sharpest tool in the box. I've always been the one with the brains".

Up until this point the others had had very little input. Ron and Charlie were just glad that all they'd lost was the money, Bunny and Judy were more interested in kids names and baby talk, Ken and Steve didn't say much and Rudy spent most of the time stoned, so it was surprising when he suddenly piped up.

"So you think you going to pull this off easy enough and them Russians just walk away with all the money"?

"We'll pull it off alright", said Jack, "but it's going to be far from easy. The timing's got to be spot on. One fuck up and we all go down".

"I like to see that woman and Ray get fucked for what they do to I".

"And what did they do to 'I' then"?

"I had a good ting going till she come along and ruin it all".

"That's right. You fucked off to Jamaica after you double crossed your brothers".

"They were not my brothers; they were bad men".

"How the fuck did she get to you in Jamaica? I know she's good, but fuck me, you'd think you would have been safe over there".

"The damn woman didn't need to come over. Ray told Winston where I was".

"And who's this Winston then"?

"He's the son of one who got killed by the police".

"So what was you doing in Jamaica then"?

"I had a nice hotel before Winston found me, then we used it as a base for Winston's drug smuggling. We were putting the drugs in the holiday makers' cases, then when they got home Winston's boys came to the house and took them".

"So what went wrong"?

"I put two packs of cocaine in a policeman's case. The next I knew my hotel was burning and I was back on a boat heading here to hide from Winston".

"Well, you won't get any sympathy from me. You deserve all you get and I hope Winston finds you".

"Maybe he will, maybe he won't. Maybe I can sort tings out with Winston". Rudy just sat back and smiled. He wasn't bothered by Jack at all. Jack took charge this time.

"Right, as much as I'd like to sit around talking to you boys, there's not a lot of time left. How have you left it with the Russians Jim"?

"I've got to go back tonight to let them know".

"Right. Me and Roger will come with you".

"I'd better get back or she'll get suspicious if I don't ask what's going on", that was Vinny's role sorted.

"Is there anything me and Steve can do"? asked Ken.

"No. You stay here and when we've had our meeting with the Russians, Jim will join you".

"No. I want to be there when she cops it. That bitch killed Tracy", I was surprised at the venom in my own voice. Jack wasn't going to indulge me though.

"Get over it Jim. When are you gonna learn that you're not a fucking gangster? You're a nice enough bloke that always seems to be in the wrong place at the wrong time. Don't you worry about Doreen – she'll get what's coming to her". Jack was right. I was out of my depth with all this gangster shit, but I just wanted to see Doreen die. I wanted her to die thinking it was because of what she did to Tracy and not some poxy Russian deal that went wrong.

We set off for London at four, arriving at the Russians' ten minutes early. I approached the intercom by the gate and I weren't as nervous as the first time I went there. I suppose having Roger and Jack to back me up helped.

I spoke to Nadia and explained who Jack and Roger were and she let us in. We went into the house and there were six big Russians all dressed in suits. They searched us, then sat us all down round a big table. Nadia kicked off the proceedings.

"So Jimmy, can we do business"? Jack didn't let me answer.

"Yeah, we can do business. We can give you five mill in cash and five in bank bonds, but you take out all of them for that. We're not sure if Vinny will be there and, if he is, I don't want him harmed".

"I know Vinny. I will be there. When and where is the exchange"?

"We don't know yet. As soon as we do, Jimmy will contact you".

We left the Russians and went back to Jack's place. It was the first time I'd been there. It was this big, four storey house in Kensington. We were there a couple of hours when Doreen rang. Jack put the phone on speaker so we could all hear her.

"Right, I'll keep it short. All the paperwork my end has been done, so Alex will be round to you later tonight to go over what we need".

"I'm telling you now, if a hair on Helen's head is harmed..." Jack played his part convincingly.

"Shut up, your precious daughter's fine. Now listen, you and only you, will come to Unit Sixteen, Botany Bay Trading Estate in Stevenage at eleven on Thursday night. You sign on the dotted line and you walk away with your daughter, but if anyone else is with you, then Helen will have an unfortunate accident with a glass of acid. Understood".

"I'll be there".

The phone went dead. There was silence for a minute and I started feeling a bit edgy and nervous.

"Shall I ring Nadia"? I asked, desperate to do something, to keep the momentum.

"Don't do nothing until I've spoken to Vinny. Give him a bell and get him round here"

Vinny turned up an hour later and Jack pounced on him immediately.

"Right son, I've spoken to Doreen and we're exchanging Thursday night at eleven".

"Whereabout's? Is it the unit"?

"Yeah. Number sixteen".

"I know it. That's where I took her".

"So what's it like"?

"It's in the middle of nowhere. I'll drive you there if you want".

"We'll do it tomorrow. Hire a van 'cos I don't want to risk her seeing us".

"Yeah, no problem. There's vans in and out that site all day".

"Has she said anything to you yet"? Roger wanted to know.

"No. I rang her and she just said I'd know when it was over".

"You'll know alright. As soon as she gets what she wants, that's it for you son", Jack predicted ominously.

Vinny took Jack there the next day while I went home. He came round later that night to let me know the details.

"So what's 'appening then"? I asked him.

"Right, you'll need to take Nadia and one of her blokes to see the layout. There's no way the Russians can get to that unit without them knowing, so they'll have to wait off the site and ambush them when they leave. There's only one way in and out, so it won't be hard".

"I don't trust her. If she's that much of a psycho, what's to stop her killing Jack and Helen as soon as he signs it over".

"She ain't stupid. She knows she'd never get away with it. Think about it. If Jack gets killed after signing over half his estate then she's first in the frame. And while they do her for that, it wouldn't take long before they link her to that copper she killed".

"Yeah, you're right. I'm just getting panicked about it all. So what do I tell the Russians then"?

"Tell them to get in position in that lane dead on eleven. All Doreen's men will either be in or around that unit".

"So when do they get their money"?

"Roger will bring it to them at their place in St John's Wood at two in the morning".

I picked Nadia up from the house in St John's Wood. I still liked her and I was pretty sure she liked me. She knew everything about me, but I knew fuck all about her, so, as we were gonna spend the next three or four hours together, I thought I'd find out.

"So Nadia, you're not a hooker, are you"?

"No. When you were driving me, you were taking me to friends and business contacts".

"Business contacts? You mean gangsters"?

"I mean very important businessman and, yes Mafia or gangsters – whatever you want to call them. My life is very complicated. You don't need to know the details. In fact, the less you know, the better for you and besides, it would take too long to explain".

"Well, we've got about four hours, so try me". She sighed.

"Fine,Jimmy. What do you know about Russia"?

"It's fucking huge. I'm not sure, but is it still Communist"?

"No. Not since the wall came down in ninety-one".

"It gets really cold in the winter and there's fucking big bears living in the woods".

Nadia laughed and started to relax.

"Yes, and tigers too, but it's not the bears and tigers you should be scared of".

"You're right there. I nearly shit myself when those two geezers pulled me out the car".

"Russia is a very corrupt country run by organized criminal groups and I belong to one of those groups".

"So there's not like one main man then, like the Italians? You know, like the Godfather"?

"No, there are many; hundreds, thousands even. It is very complicated. Each group specialises in different criminal activities, such as money laundering, racketeering, extortion, arms trafficking and murder".

"So your group's speciality is drugs and prostitution".

"That's correct".

"How did you get into all this then"?

"When America expanded its immigration policies and allowed Soviet Jews to enter their country, it was the perfect opportunity for many Soviet criminals to enter too. I moved to America with my parents in 1983. My father was a leading figure in Brooklyn in an area known as Brighton Beach".

"What? There's a Brighton Beach in America"?

"Yes. Like I said – in Brooklyn".

"So your Dad was a bit of a gangster, was he"?

"Yes. By 1990 he had set up a very lucrative heroin business. We realised the millions that can be made from drugs, but so did many others and a Mafia turf war erupted. There were many killed, including my mother, so my father and I went back to Russia and concentrated on the European market. We spent four years establishing our trade in Europe".

"You make it sound like a proper business".

"There are very few businesses in Russia that are run legitimately; most people can be bought in some way or other".

"So were you selling your heroin over here"?

"Not directly, but yes, our heroin was destined for here and we were making a lot of money, but then suddenly demand dropped off, which meant the dealers were buying from another source. We spent many months trying to figure it out. Lots of people lost their lives, but we still couldn't get to the bottom of it. Eventually we traced it back to Afghanistan and India. We sent four men to India and that's when we found out about the container coming directly to England".

"So you knew all along"? I couldn't believe it.

"We knew how the drugs were getting here, but we didn't know who was behind it. It didn't take us long to track Nadine down".

"So what's gonna happen to her"?

"She's dead".

"Fucking 'ell. You don't mess about".

"This Doreen woman had no idea who she was messing with".

"She did. She well and truly set us up. Look how close we were to your lot killing us".

"It's not over yet. They still might".

"You serious"?

"Very. As long as everything goes to plan, you will be alright, but if it doesn't then I can't help you. Now we know who's behind it we can eliminate the problem. You are very lucky to still be alive; we were looking for you and your friends for several days".

"So if you'd found us, you were gonna kill us"?

"Yes"

"Then what"?

"Then we would have gone back home. Our only purpose

here is to stop the direct importation of heroin from India".

When she told me how close we all were to getting killed, she didn't give a shit. She said it like it was another day at the office. Death was no big deal to her.

"Tell me about this Jack who you brought to see us".

"Jack's alright. He's no gangster; he's more of a business man".

"And what business is that"?

"Property. He used to own all the bookies in London and most of the clubs, but he sold them all off and bought houses that he rents out".

"That's interesting".

"Why"?

"Do you think he built up his property empire legitimately"?

"No. Back in the sixties and seventies, he was probably giving out back handers left, right and centre".

"So he has many contacts then"?

"No. Not anymore. All he's interested in is playing golf and spending time with his family. His daughter means the world to him". I didn't like the way she was interested in Jack's business, so I changed the subject.

"So you don't fancy a normal life then? You know, husband, kids, that sort of thing"?

"Maybe one day I will settle down, but not yet. I like the excitement"?

"Yeah, normal ain't exciting, but I tell you what – when this is all over, that's exactly what I want".

It took us about an hour to get to where Helen was being held. We drove up and down a few times, then headed back to London. I dropped her off then went back to join the others in Brighton to wait it out. Charlie and Ron didn't want nothing to do with it, so they went back home. When I told the others the full plan, they thought it was great and so did I. It was fucking clever when you thought about it; we were paying the Russians to kill Doreen and using her money to do it.

Vinny was at Judy's when I got there and Judy had booked a table for me, her, Bunny and Vinny at her favourite restaurant. Ken and Steven stayed in and played pool and Rudy decided to go and stay with an old aunt in London. Rudy had just as much to worry about as us. In fact, he had more; them Jamaicans he pissed off were just as bad as the Russians.

While the girls were upstairs I had a chance to chat to Vinny. He started quizzing me about Nadia straight away.

"So how did you get on with the Russian? Do you trust her"?

"I dunno mate. She's hard to read. When I first met her and I was driving her around, I thought she was alright. A bit of a nosy cow, but I really liked her and I thought she liked me".

"You wanted to give her one, didn't yer"?

"Yeah. Course I did – she's stunning, but it weren't just that; I really liked her".

"You really are a fucking mug sometimes, Jim. What did I tell yer and I bet Dave said the same? Them girls are the most manipulative you'll ever meet. They know exactly how to feed a bloke's ego; they suck you in and then spew you out once you've got fuck all to offer them".

"Yeah, I can see why they do that with the clients, but I weren't paying her, was I"?

"She weren't after your money. She was after info and you probably told her everything she needed to know".

"Yeah, I did, but most of it was personal stuff. You know what though? None of it sunk in. She told me they'd been looking for us and if we hadn't have come down here, we'd be fucking dead".

"Yeah, Roger was right – that Doreen is one clever bitch".

"How can someone take the time to get to know you one

minute, then be ready to blow your brains out the next"?

"Get over it, Jim. She was over here for one reason only and that was to find out who was muscling in on their business. She found out and the next step was to eliminate the problem. Hopefully you've done enough to convince her you've got fuck all to do with it, but the other thing you've got to worry about is you now know a lot about their operation, they might decide to take you out just to cover their tracks".

"No, I don't think so. She said as long as there's no problem we'll be alright".

"Let's hope so mate, right, I've done with talking about this shit, fucking hell, Jim. I'm gonna be a Dad"!

"No need to ask how you feel about it. You're well chuffed, ain't yer"?

"Yeah, I am".

"I never had you down as Dad material, I have to say".

"No, nor did I, to be honest, it's not the kid I'm so chuffed about, it's more to do with the fact that me and Bunny have got a future, the kid will tie us together, especially now Dave's gone as well".

"I'll miss Dave. I knew him a long time".

"I'm sorry Jim. I know you went way back and he was your best mate, but it just makes it easier for me not having him around".

"You didn't have anything to worry about, Bunny had made her mind up. Her and Dave were definitely over".

"It's fucking crazy, ain't it? In the space of a few days I find out I'm gonna be a Dad, and I've got a Dad, and you, yer fucker, you knew all along".

"I came close to telling you a few times, but I promised Jack I wouldn't. I don't know why he didn't want you to know, but he obviously had his reasons".

"When this is over me and Jack have got a lot to talk about. I know Helen's his number one, but I'll be giving him his first grandchild".

"Well let's hope he gets her back in one piece".

"Yeah he will. Doreen's a bit psycho, but she ain't fucking stupid. Anyway, Jim, what do yer reckon about tonight"? Vinny changed the subject.

"I reckon I'm fucking starving. Why? What do you mean"?

"You know Bunny's trying to set you up with Judy, don't yer"?

"Yeah, as it 'appens, I did notice that".

"Well, you interested or what"?

"Yeah I am, the trouble is, I've always looked at her as a mate and I can tell yer – over the years she's been a fucking good one. Since I've been down here though, I've really started to fancy her, it's weird, ain't it? She seems to have got better with age, the other night when we went out she looked well tasty in that dog-toothed check skirt".

"Yeah Bunny reckons she had loads of nice gear, but she wore that 'cos she knows you like all that old sixties clobber. So you gonna make a move then? I reckon she's well up for it".

"She might well be, but I ain't. Not until this lot's sorted out".

"Look mate, we've done all we can, so let's just go out tonight, have some fun, and forget about it".

"I can't. I'm worried fucking sick".

"You'll be alright, trust me, once you've got a few beers down your neck you'll be fine".

It took the girls about an hour and half to get ready and in that time we downed about four pints. I hadn't eaten all day so I felt well pissed.

When they finally appeared in the room, they looked stunning, but Judy definitely had the edge on Bunny. Years of partying hard with Dave had clearly taken its toll. Too much booze, drugs, late nights and fags was etched into her face. Don't get me wrong; she was still stunning, but Judy looked ten years younger.

Since Tracy died, drink had a different effect on me. I used to get pissed, dance all night and make a prat of myself, but that was when I was happy and without a care in the world. When Tracy died, I would sit and drink on my own. Just as I could feel myself getting pissed I would remember all the good times we shared and it made me happy, but then the more I drank, the further I would slip into depression. When Judy walked in that room and smiled at me, I was at that happy point and I had flash backs to when Tracy used to stand there and say "well, what do you think?" It was a defining moment for me and tears were starting to well up in my eyes. I could feel myself getting all emotional and before I could say how lovely she looked, she said,

"What do you think"?

I was speechless. I could feel a tear running down my cheek and, before it reached the bottom, Judy came over and gave me a cuddle. Bunny grabbed Vinny and left us. Me and Judy spent all night talking. At first I was confused as I wasn't sure what I was feeling. I thought it was guilt, but when I woke up in the morning lying next to Judy, I knew it was love. We stayed in bed all morning. Her room had the perfect view of the beach and pier and I wanted the moment to last forever. I made a decision right then that when it was all over, this is where I wanted to stay. Here in Brighton, with Judy.

We eventually came down and joined the others at about eleven and Ken well and truly burst my bubble.

"Tonight's the night, let's hope you've done enough to convince that Russian bird to save us all. I hope for your sake, Vinny, that Jack gets Helen back alright".

"So do I", said Steve.

"I ain't worried", said Vinny. "She's alright"

"We'll be alright", I tried to encourage everyone. "Nadia

guaranteed that as long as everything goes to plan and they get their money, we won't see or hear from them again".

"So who's doing the drop with the money"? asked Ken.

"Roger", I told him.

"And you trust him? What if he decides to disappear"?

"He's got a point, Jim". Vinny backed up Ken.

"No, he won't. I know him".

Ken was starting to piss me off, so me and Judy went for a walk along the beach. I loved the crunching sound of the pebbles under our feet and the smell of the seaweed drying out in the midday sun. *The Who* once sang "nothing is planned by the sea and the sand". Well, there ain't much sand here in Brighton, but I've planned plenty sitting here by the sea. The sound of the waves crashing down on the pebbles blocked out all other noises that would distract me from my train of deep thought. I've always had a special place that I could escape to when things weren't going quite right in my life. When I was a kid, I'd sit on the railway embankment for hours locked in my imaginary world. Sometimes I would feel happy and smile to myself, then other times I felt angry and frustrated. When I felt like that I would smash the discarded bottles left lying around by the winos up against the bridge wall. The smashing noise and seeing bits of shattered glass flying everywhere made me feel better. I've never really known if I am truly nuts, or it's just something my Dad instilled in my brain from a young age. There is, without a doubt, a fucking nutty gene that runs through our family and when I was popping pills left right and centre back in sixty-five, it made me very confused and it didn't help matters. Going inside was probably what saved me. Locked in a cell every night for eight years gives you plenty of time to get your head round things. When I got out and my Mum and Dad picked me up, I was a completely different person. I came down here and sat on the beach and I knew I wasn't fucking nuts. It was the years of constantly being told it by my

Dad that made me feel it. Tracy was the part of the jigsaw that made my life complete. Being in love is the best feeling in the world and when she died I'd considered myself lucky that I had discovered love. Some people never find that. It would have been so easy to have ended it all when she died and, believe me, I came close a couple of times. But there I was, sitting in my special place with Judy, feeling like I did back then when I first clapped eyes on Tracy and we were making plans for our future.

"So Jim, have I got you at last"? she asked me.

"You've always fancied me, ain't yer"?

"You know I have".

"I've got to be honest; it ain't always been like that for me. I've always liked yer and cared about yer, but there was never that real spark and when I got out the nick and went to see you in America with all your hippy mates I couldn't wait to get back home".

"You never really got what we was about, did you"?

"I sort of did. No, in fact, I think I did subconsciously because I'm still here now. That's down to you and your philosophy on life".

"You know how I feel about you, but are you sure how you feel about me? I'm not just filling that void left in your life by Tracy am I"?

"No, you're not, but I don't blame you for thinking that. While we've been sitting here I've been thinking the same thing and I'm a hundred per cent sure what I felt last night, what I feel now, is love. It's the same feeling I've only ever experienced once before and that was with Tracy. When this is all over I want to get rid of the club and the shop, sell the house, and move down here with you. I want a completely new start".

"That sounds good to me. Can you cook"?

"Yeah, why"?

"We'll make a great team running the B and B. You can do all the cooking and I'll sort all the other stuff out".

"Nah, bollocks to that! I ain't running a fucking B and B. I was thinking of opening a clothes shop or a small club. Your place is great, but I don't wanna share it with a load of strangers".

"It's a big place for just two of us".

"Well perhaps we can convert it into separate apartments and we take the top floor. We'll think of something, but I definitely ain't running a poxy B and B".

"Sounds good to me".

"So how do you think Bunny will cope with a kid"?

"I think she'll be alright. She's over the moon".

"Yeah, so is Vinny. Rather him than me".

"You never fancied kids of your own then"?

"Nah, what about you"?

"If things had been different, yeah, but I'm well over it now".

"Good. Glad to hear it".

We talked for hours. I think initially she was a bit taken back with my response to running a B and B, but bollocks to that. How uncool? I know I wanted a new start, but knocking up fried breakfasts for people away on dirty weekends ain't what I had in mind.

We got back to Judy's at about seven thirty, which was just in time to catch Vinny and Bunny going out. We talked them into waiting for us and we all went out an hour later.

It was a tense evening. The girls were talking a load of shit about babies and stuff, while me and Vinny were coming up with contingency plans in case it all went tits up. We felt pretty sure Jack would get Helen alright, but the Russians were an unknown entity to us. Our lives were worlds apart; They came from a country that thrived on corruption, crime and cold-blooded murder. When Nadia said I was only alive because they couldn't find me, it turned my blood to ice.

When we got back at about eleven, Ken and Steve were watching a video. The girls sat out on the balcony with a bottle of wine and we sat with Ken and Steve with one eye on the film and the other on the clock. Dead on twelve the phone rang, Ken hit the pause on the video machine, Judy and Bunny came in from the balcony, while me and Vinny just stared at the phone.

"Well fucking answer it then", demanded Ken.

"You do the honours, Jim", said Vinny.

It was Jack saying he'd got Helen and she was okay. He said there was no sign of the Russians and he was heading home. Ken gave Steve a hug and Judy popped open a bottle of champagne, but me and Vinny knew it was far from over. We weren't popping no champagne corks until we got that call from Roger saying he'd paid the Russians and we were in the clear. We were expecting Roger's call at about two, so when the phone rang again forty minutes later it stopped us in our tracks. I answered it again. It was Nadia. She said that Doreen and six of her men went down without a fight; they weren't even armed. I put the phone down and you could have heard a pin drop. I wanted to wind them up, but I didn't prolong it for a second. Vinny grinned and shook my hand, Judy gave me a hug, and I popped the next bottle of champagne. Steve put some music on and the party began. We all sat around laughing and joking and I called Jack at about one fifteen to tell him. he told me that Roger was on his way to drop the money.

The phone rang again at two forty-five and Judy turned the music down. We were all a bit pissed and totally relaxed, but when I picked the phone up it was Nadia, not Roger. It completely threw me out and the others could tell by my reaction that something was wrong. They switched the music off and just stared. Nadia was telling me what had happened, but it weren't quite registering in my head. I put the receiver down and just put my head in my hands in stunned disbelief at what I'd just heard.

"That weren't Roger telling us it's all sorted, was it"? asked Vinny.

"No. No it fucking weren't".

"What's going on Jim? Who was it"? Bunny's voice had gone all high-pitched and squeaky.

"Yeah. Who the fuck was it"? Ken practically shouted.

I felt dizzy and sick and I was trying to come up with answers before I'd even told them what had happened.

"Come on Jim. You're scaring us", Judy brought me back to reality and I knew I just had to tell them.

"That was Nadia. She said Roger pulled up at the gate, got out the motor to press the intercom, but before he could get back in his car a BMW pulled up, three blacks got out and shot him, then drove off with the money".

"You're serious, ain't yer? You're not winding us up"? Steven was clinging to a last bit of hope.

"No, mate. I'm not winding you up".

"Fucking blacks. How did they know what was in that motor"? Ken asked nobody in particular.

"It don't take a lot of working out does it? It weren't a random mugging", said Vinny.

"Fucking Rudy. That dodgy fucker has turned us over", I said. It was the only explanation.

"What else did she say"? asked Vinny.

"She's well pissed off. They've had to get their gear together and shoot down to their other place near Gatwick".

"Well, what are they so worried about"? Ken asked.

"I don't believe you just said that, you twat", spat Vinny. I answered for him.

"Fucking hell, Ken. Think about it. The Old Bill turn up to a dead gangster outside a Russian's house with four or five Russians sitting in there, drinking vodka, with their guns still hot from shooting seven other gangsters a couple of hours earlier. Can you see the connection"?

"How you left it with her"? asked Vinny.

"She's steaming mate. She thinks we've used them to get rid of Doreen, taken the money and set them up with the Old Bill".

"I suppose when you look at it from her point of view you'd think the same", said Steve.

"What we gonna do"? asked Bunny, voicing the question on everyone's lips.

"The first thing we'd better do is warn Jack", Vinny decided.

I rang Jack and told him, but he didn't give a shit about our predicament. He just said he would be going off the radar until it all blew over. I told them the rest of the bad news.

"She said she's gonna call tomorrow and she wants answers".

"Well we' better give her some, starting with Rudy's number and that photo Judy took of you all", suggested Ken.

"We can't do that", I said.

"We fucking can", said Vinny. "I don't give a fuck what he done to Roger, but that black bastard's put us all in the shit".

"Vinny's right. I can't believe he'd do that to us". That was Judy for you, always wanting to trust people, even when they stabbed you in the back. I tried to think like her, to see his side.

"I suppose you gotta look at it from his point of view. We were all so concerned about saving our own arses that we didn't stop to think of him and his problem with that drug dealer Winston. You think about it – he's well in the clear now".

"He fucking ain't", growled Ken. "You wait till I get hold of him".

"Unless I can convince Nadia, you won't get the chance".

Fucking Rudy. Who would have thought it? All the time he was sitting there stoned he'd clocked exactly what was going on, the crafty git. I didn't know whether to laugh or cry 'cos we were back in exactly the same position that Doreen had put us in. The midday news was full of it. The seven bodies that were found in a lane in Stevenage were linked to Roger's shooting in London and the police released descriptions of the three black blokes responsible thanks to CCTV cameras, but none of them were described as a Bob Marley look-alike.

Nadia rang the next day and wanted to meet me. If it had been at the house I used to take her to, I wouldn't have gone, but instead it was at the Hilton Hotel, in the bar. I took the photo of Rudy and I was gonna tell her everything. I walked into the bar and she was sitting there with a huge geezer.

"Hello Jim".

"Alright. Who's this"?

"My name is Vladimir. Nadia has told me all about you".

"All good, I hope"?

"You are very lucky she thinks a lot of you. If it were down to me, you and your friends would be dead. It would have been no problem stopping off at Brighton yesterday to finish the job".

"You know where we were staying"? I gulped.

"We know a lot more than you think Jimmy", said Nadia.

I went to give her the photo of Rudy and explain what he'd done, but she wasn't interested.

"It's not important", said Vladimir. "Our business here is concluded as we are satisfied the problem has been eliminated".

"We fly back tonight", Nadia added.

"What about the money"? I was confused. They were gonna let us get away without paying?

"It was never about the money, Jimmy. Doreen had chosen a very important time to get involved with the heroin trade. Like I explained to you, Jimmy, there are many well-organised groups in Russia and we had to be satisfied that the threat to us wasn't coming from one of these such groups. A lot of lives have been lost and Doreen has paid the price".

"So that's it? It's definitely over"?

"Yes", she confirmed.

I rang Judy and told her to put another couple of bottles on ice 'cos it was finally all over. When I got back to Brighton, I thought we'd all go out and celebrate but the truth was we'd all had enough; we were exhausted. Bunny and Vinny had a lot to sort out with the agency and Dave's funeral, Steven wanted to get back to his Mum, and Ken wanted to track Rudy down and kill him. Ken was never that keen on Rudy, so he was well pissed off that out of all the shit that had gone on Rudy came out on top of everyone. I'd got passed the anger and saw the funny side of it. I decided to stay with Judy until Dave's funeral.

It didn't take long for the police to release Dave's body and it was all pretty clean cut. He was wanted by them, he got pissed, decided to end it all and jumped off a cliff. Bunny decided to have the funeral in Brighton two weeks later, which I was quite happy with. It gave me a chance to really explore the town. I'd spent plenty of weekends and day trips here, but now I was thinking of settling here I could look round at potential businesses. I rode round Brighton and Hove for ages on my scooter, but I weren't too sure what I wanted. Then I came across an old derelict pub between Brighton and Hove, all boarded up, but huge. It had a big function room round the back and a nice big plot of land. I know I could have done the same to that place as I did with The Punch Bowl. If it worked in Stevenage then it would definitely work in the seaside town, which many regard as the Mod favourite.

I got myself some fish and chips and sat on a bench opposite. I gave it a lot of thought and all the good times came flooding back from way back, to the early seventies when I bought the shit-hole of a boozer called The Punch Bowl. It was a massive part of my life. It didn't take me long to get past the happy memories and start thinking of all the grief that it had caused me. By the time I'd got to the bits of crumbled batter and soggy chips swimming round in a pool of vinegar, I'd actually started to hate The Punch Bowl. In fact, I never wanted to see it again. I threw what was left of my fish and chips to the seagulls and got back on my scooter. What started out as a really positive and happy day had now turned into a nightmare of anger and self-doubt. I was beginning to question what I was all about. I mean, there I was, knocking on the door of fifty and I was still riding a scooter. Was the reason that I owned a club and I had to be seen as a Mod because they were my paying customers, or did I really love being who I was?. I seemed to be riding for ages and, before I knew it, I was the other side of Brighton at Beachy Head. The cliffs are hundreds of feet high and it attracts a lot of tourists. There's always a mobile burger van or ice cream float in the car park, so I parked up and got a coffee. As I turned from the coffee bar and walked towards my scooter, a bloke with a Labrador walked over and started looking at it.

"I used to have one of these back in the sixties", he said.

"What did you have then"?

"An LI150. You don't see many about any more. Can you still get the parts for them"?

"There's still plenty about. The Mod scene is still going strong".

"I used to love riding round in the summer".

"Why don't you get another one then"?

"I'm too old for all that, mate. I've got a wife, kids and mortgage".

He laughed as he said it and walked off with his dog. It was only a two-minute conversation, but it was enough to put all them doubts I'd been having to bed. I mean, there was a geezer the same age as me, and it was like he'd given up on life. The way he said about the wife, kids and mortgage, was like his life was over. He couldn't have fun anymore. How fucking sad is that? Nah, bollocks to that. I never have, and never will give a shit what people think. I don't hold with the idea that when you get to a certain age you can't do this, or you've gotta act in a certain way. I drank my coffee and headed back to Brighton. Talking to that sad git done me good and I sat proud on my scooter knowing I weren't ready for the pipe and slippers yet.

I got back to Judy's and told her about my day and the conversation with the boring geezer and, while she agreed that there shouldn't be limits on what you should or shouldn't do at a certain age, she said she'd got out the stage of wanting to party every weekend. She said she wanted to travel more and explore the world instead. It's not something I'd really thought about, but listening to how passionately she spoke about it and some of the things she wanted to see and experience, I thought I fancied some of that too. We chatted for ages and she made me realise that there was more to life than the bubble I'd been living in over the last twenty odd years.

Judy had obviously done a lot of talking with Bunny and Bunny had mentioned to her what I said about a clothes shop. To be honest, with all the excitement of recent events, I'd forgotten all about it; my head was all over the place. Judy came up with a great idea though: her place was at the end of a parade of shops, so we could convert downstairs to a shop and turn the three floors into apartments, with us living at the top. That way we had a guaranteed income if the shop was a bit slow to take off. Well, that was it. I made my mind up that The Punch Bowl and the bike shop were going.

The two weeks leading up to Dave's funeral went quickly. In that time we'd all had time to reflect on what had been an absolute fucking nightmare. Dave never had any family and the only friends he had were us, so the funeral gave us a chance to talk and see where we would go from there.

CHAPTER 9

THE FUNERAL AND BEYOND

There was me, Judy, Bunny, Vinny, Ron, Charlie, Steve and Ken. It was a bit of a sad, pathetic funeral, which Ken said summed Dave up, but it didn't. I knew Dave a long time and he'd given me a lot of good advice over the years and been a good friend when I needed one. Ron said he was a selfish bastard for topping himself and that seemed to be the general consensus with regards to suicide, but I thought, in Dave's case, it was the right thing to do. I certainly didn't feel betrayed by his decision and, seeing how happy Bunny was, neither did she.

Losing Tracy was the closest I'd come to doing it, and if she'd gone off with someone else and found happiness I think that would have been worse than her dying so I probably would have ended up on the beach at Beachy Head.

"Well thanks everyone for coming", announced Bunny.

"That's alright", said Charlie.

"Why didn't Rudy turn up then"? asked Ron, the stupid fucker.

"Jim's not filled you in then? Rudy fucked of with five million quid", Ken answered him.

"What"? Charlie was obviously not registering yet.

"We don't know that", said Judy.

"What yer talking about? He disappeared two days before Roger got his brains blown out by three coons. Of course we fucking do", argued Ken.

"What's he going on about Jim"? Ron asked. I sighed, not wanting to go over it agian.

"Everything went to plan: Jack got Helen back and Roger was going to pay off the Russians, but he got jumped by three black geezers and we ain't heard nothing from Rudy since".

"So you didn't have any luck finding him then Ken", Vinny asked.

"Nah, he's fucking gone. No-one's seen or heard from him".

"That's Rudy; master of the disappearing act", chuckled Charlie. "Do you remember back in sixty-five, when we needed pills for Brighton and he fucked off for ages, then all of a sudden he pops back up again"?

"Yeah I remember", I said. "I think we searched the whole of South London".

"We ended up buying a load off dodgy pills from that geezer down The Cherry Tree", he finished.

"That's right. Dave ended up putting the geezer's windscreen through", I definitely remembered that part.

"Yeah, fucking nutter. He always went over the top", muttered Ron, making us all laugh.

"So Rudy came out on top of all of us then"? Charlie wanted to get it straight.

"I don't know about that. Me and Vinny are having a baby", said Bunny, with this huge grin on her face from ear to ear.

"Best of luck with that one. Me and my missus had kids a lot younger than you are and they're fucking hard work". Charlie was such a dick sometimes.

"Yeah, fuck that", Ron followed suit.

"Don't listen to them. I think it's great and you'll be fine", soothed Judy.

"Yeah, I can't wait. What have you and Jim got planned then?"

"Shall I tell them Jim, or you"? asked Judy.

"Fuck me. You ain't knocked up as well, are yer"? Ken spluttered.

"Don't be fucking daft. We've only been together a couple of weeks".

"So what's your plans, Jim"? Steve persisted.

"I'm selling up; the shop, the club – I want a new start down here".

"Great. What about us"?

"Ken, I don't give a fuck about you. Until the shop's sold, Steven is in charge. I don't want you 'aving nothing to do with it other than fixing bikes and you're fucking lucky I'm letting you do that".

"Is that right? Well, bollocks to you. I don't need your fucking charity. I ain't working on poxy scooters for fuck all".

"Yeah, that's right. You only showed an interest because you was ripping Jim off and now there's nothing in it for you, you don't wanna know". I could tell Steve was hurt by his Dad's comments.

"Look son, I enjoyed working with yer, but you're right; it served a purpose so now it's time I moved on".

"Where you gonna go"? I asked him.

"Your sister don't want anything to do with me no more, so I'm going to stay with a mate up North. He's got a Triumph dealership up there, so I can get back to what I love; fixing real bikes".

Ken left straight away, which made me think he only came to the funeral to see if there was anything in it for him. It's a shame 'cos I've known Ken longer than Dave, but you can only give someone so many chances and what he done was bang out of order. Steven weren't sorted though.

"It ain't gonna be easy selling the shop, Jim. Is there any chance I can buy it and pay you monthly – like a mortgage"?

"Yeah. I reckon we can sort something out". I'd be glad for Steve to take it on.

"Now your old man's fucked off, you'll need someone who knows their way round a scooter. Any chance of a job"? Charlie got in there before Ron had even opened his mouth.

"Yeah, of course". Steve was only too happy to have some help.

"What about our building business"? Ron whinged.

"What fucking business? Anyway, I've had enough of the building game; knocking up shit all day and digging holes. I ain't getting any younger and my back's fucked".

"Fucking age", I scoffed. "You ain't fifty yet".

"I know and I can still walk straight. I want to get out before I end up like a knackered old Paddy".

Vinny had a good idea to help Ron out, though, so he soon stopped his complaining.

"I tell yer what, Ron – I need someone I can trust to help run the agency. Once Bunny's had the baby, I'm not working every night; you can manage it for me".

"Yeah, great. I'll take you up on that".

"So Jim, you definitely want out of The Punch Bowl"? Vinny checked.

"Yeah".

"Well, so do I".

"It'll be a shame 'cos I've really started to turn it around". Steve was relentless with his fucking problems, but I didn't mind. He was my nephew, after all.

"I'm quite happy to let you carry on. What about you, Vinny"?

"You know me; I ain't had fuck all to do with it for ages. If you can make a go of it then carry on. All I want to see is a nice, healthy profit at the end of the year. If I don't then we'll review the situation".

"You will. Trust me", Steve reassured us.

"Good". I said.

"Steve, have you heard anything from Helen yet"? Vinny wanted to know.

"No".

"No, I ain't heard nothing from Jack either".

"So Judy, what are you two gonna get up to down here"? Bunny switched the subject back onto our life plan.

"We've had an architect look at this place and as soon as the plans for converting it are approved, me and Jim are going on a very long holiday until the builders are finished".

"I can put you in touch with some good builders", offered Charlie. "What do you want doing"?

"We're 'aving all the first floor knocked through and made into a shop and the other floors into apartments", I told him.

"That'll cost yer", said Ron.

"I've still got a fair bit stashed, so we should be alright".

"So where you going to disappear to"? asked Bunny.

"I thought we'd hire a villa in Portugal. Me and Tracy always talked about it, so I thought I'd see if reality lives up to the dream".

"You can't do that! It seems wrong. Pick somewhere else like Spain or Italy… anywhere but Portugal". Bunny was shocked.

"You're right. I weren't thinking".

"I don't mind where it is as long as it's hot and peaceful". I felt a wave of love for Judy when she said that.

We carried on talking well into the night. The next day, me and Judy went for a walk along the seafront and were summing up the last six months. We came to the conclusion that it could have been a lot worse. Judy was a very philosophical person and she had an answer for everything. She believed in karma and that everything happened for a reason. She could take good out of the most horrendous of circumstances and she started with Roger. He was a gangster who'd spent his life bribing and blackmailing and was responsible for hundreds of lives ruined by the drugs he dealt. Would he be missed? No. Then there was Rudy – another dealer who had spent his life living off the profits of the pain and misery drugs can cause. We don't know exactly what happened to him, but it's a pretty safe bet that Winston caught up with him. Ken got what he deserved; he was greedy and put us all in a lot of danger. Ron and Charlie are harmless plodders and now they're both happy. Dave dying was the strangest twist because, as much as a mate he was, seeing Bunny as happy as she was made his death seem like the right thing. It seems crazy saying it, but Dave really did have a fantastic life. He had it all: fast cars, boats, sex with some of the most stunning women, travelling and staying in first class hotels, and the love of a beautiful woman, which was the one thing he couldn't live without. That left me. I was still feeling really guilty over Tracy's death. Judy even had an answer to that, but to be honest I didn't want to know. All I knew was I loved her and I'd like her back, but that it weren't gonna happen. Life goes on. Like Judy said, life is about chapters and I feel lucky to have someone like Judy to start the next one with.

They say time flies when you're having fun and it certainly did for me and Judy. We spent the next three years travelling. It done me a world of good 'cos before Tracy died, my whole life centred around The Punch Bowl and the Mod scene. I really got off on being one of the faces. It was something I craved in the sixties and there I was, well into my forties owning a scooter shop and one of the liveliest Mod clubs in the South of England. It was like I had celebrity status. I was liked and respected for all the right reasons and it was fair to say it took over my life. Tracy was happy to let me indulge my love of everything Mod.

Judy, on the other hand, wasn't. She accepted I was always gonna be part of the scene, but she gradually weaned me off of it. We was always flitting off somewhere exotic. She opened my eyes and showed me there was more to life.

The shop was doing really well. We specialised in high quality designer clothes and we had a tailor working full time on made-to-measure suits. Our original plan was to live in the top apartment, but we ended up letting all three out. We bought a nice detached house just outside Brighton 'cos Judy wanted a dog and I needed a garage for my collection of scooters.

It's bizarre how things turned out. Jack Warren was always a very aloof, unapproachable bloke. He was hugely wealthy and successful, but he mellowed with age and turned out to be a really nice geezer. I suppose he had to really because we was all like one big family in the end. Steve married Helen and he was my nephew, Vinny married Bunny, me and Judy were Godparents to their daughter, which was Jack's grandchild so there was plenty of special occasions when we all met up.

Money was never an issue; we always had plenty. Jack bought the scooter shop off me and gave it to Steven and Helen as a wedding present and Vinny was making an absolute fortune from the escort agency. Jack didn't like it 'cos he wanted Vinny to work for him, but Vinny liked to be his own boss.

Steven done really well with The Punch Bowl, so me and Vinny gave him our share of the club.

Time and age are funny. When you're a kid, time drags on and you want time to fly, so you can do all the fun things you associate with being an adult and you try to look older. Then, when you are older, time goes too quick and you want to look younger. Well the years flew by and, before I knew it, I was heading to Stevenage to celebrate my sixtieth birthday at The Punch Bowl.

It was 2007 and the Mod scooter scene was still going strong. This party was no quiet affair: we had two bands and a top DJ booked and everyone was there. We all got well pissed and had a great time. Being at The Punch Bowl brought back a lot of happy memories. The plan was to go back to Bunny and Vinny's place for a chat and to catch up on what everyone had been up to, but we were all pretty wrecked, so we all went round there the next day for a barbecue instead.

"I don't know about you lot, but Jesus I feel rough" I said, as I walked in.

"You're getting too old for it all, Jim. It's your body telling you to slow down", Steven teased.

"Is it, bollocks. A hangover's a hangover, whatever age you are".

"Yeah, you tell him love", cheered Judy.

"I dunno, he might be right. It was a great night, but I couldn't do it too often" Charlie said.

"Me neither", agreed Ron. "So, where you two off to next then"? asked Vinny.

"I fancy going a bit further. Maybe China or Thailand…" Judy though out loud.

"Yeah, I like the idea of that. There's plenty to see over there. I'd like to see the Great Wall of China and The Terracotta Army".

"I didn't know you were into all that"! Said Ron.

"Yeah, I love it. We've seen some fantastic things".

"Sod that", said Charlie. "Give me a beach and a cold beer any day".

"We do usually spend the first week chilling out then we get bored and do the sights", I explained.

"We're gonna start having more holidays now Geogia's getting older", said Bunny.

"How old is she now" Judy asked.

"She's twelve".

"You should take her to Disneyland in Florida".

"You been there, have yer"?

"Nah, Jim don't fancy it. He was put off America that time he came and stayed with me when he got out of prison".

"I don't blame him", chipped in Vinny "All that fucking Mickey Mouse and Donald Duck".

"It ain't all like that. America's fantastic. I'll get him over there one day".

Bunny turned her endless nosey questions onto Steve and Helen.

"So Steven, when are you and Helen going to have kids"? Helen's mouth fell open.

"You know, don't you"?

"Know what? You're pregnant, aren't you"?

"Yeah. I'm two months gone".

"Congratulations! Well done sis. It's a shame Dad's not around to see it". Vinny was chuffed.

"Yeah. It's a shame he died 'cos he turned out to be a sound geezer in the end", I said.

"I miss him a lot", said Helen, tears shimmering in her eyes. Vinny could see she was struggling, so he turned to me.

"So how's business then Jim? Doing all right are yer"?

"Yeah. We sell a lot of stuff mail order now. What about you"?

"Since Jack died, me and Helen have taken over the business. It was a clean fifty–fifty split".

"Fuck me. You must be well loaded now".

"Yeah, I'm doing alright. It came at the right time really".

"Why's that then"?

"The agency ain't making as much as it used to".

"What 'appened? The demand for hookers drop off, did it"?

"No, the opposite. Trouble is, agencies are popping up left, right and centre. In fact, I'm beginning to think it ain't worth the hassle".

"Well, give me first shout if you sell up", said Ron.

"Yeah. No problem".

"You never said anything to me about Helen getting half Jack's estate" I said to Steve.

"Why would I? Anyway I thought you would have known".

"We all done alright in the end, didn't we"?
Charlie snorted.

"You lot did. Me and Ron are still scraping by".

Charlie was right, I did feel a bit guilty and judging by the look on Steven's and Vinny's faces, they did as well, so I got them away from the others and had a chat.

"What do you reckon you two are worth"? I asked 'em.

"Fucking millions mate", answered Vinny smugly.

"You and Helen are. I ain't", said Steve.

"Course you are. You're married ain't yer? What's yours is hers and what's hers is yours".

"Yeah, you're right I suppose, and I do own the club and shop".

"Look, Vinny, you've just said the agency ain't worth the hassle, so why don't you just give it to Ron? He practically runs it on his own anyway".

"Yeah, you're right. It would be hard to value and sell as a business anyway. I mean, you couldn't exactly float it on the Stock Market could yer"?

"And what about the scooter shop, Steve? Why don't you give it to Charlie? Your first love is The Punch Bowl and when Helen has the baby you're gonna have to help Vinny out".
Vinny agreed with me.

"Yeah, he's got a point Steve. When Bunny had Georgia, she didn't want to do fuck all; she spent most of her time doing coffee mornings and going up the gym".

"Charlie is a good bloke and the customers love him. I'll let him have it on the condition that it's always run as a scooter shop", Steve decided.

It didn't take a lot of thinking; they were both worth an obscene amount of money. We rejoined the others to tell them. Vinny started it off.

“Right Ron, we’ve been having a bit of a chat and I’ve decided to give you the agency”.

“You serious”?

“Yeah, I am. Like I say, I don’t think I can be bothered with the hassle anymore”.

“Fucking hell. Cheers mate”.

“That’s a touch, you lucky bastard”, said Charlie.

Charlie was pleased for Ron but you could tell he was a bit gutted, so Steve didn’t drag it out too long.

“Cheer up Charlie; you’ve got a face like a spanked arse. I’m giving you the scooter shop”.

“Fuck me. I don’t know what to say”.

“Try ‘thank you’” Helen suggested, tongue in cheek.

“Yeah thanks. When did you decide that”?

“We didn’t. Steve did”.

“That’s right. I figured you ain’t gonna want to be working too much when the baby’s born, so I’d work with Vinny”.

“He’s right”, Bunny was nodding her head in approval. “When Geogia was born I just wanted to be with her all the time”.

“Yeah, you’re right I suppose”, agreed Helen.

Well, needless to say it turned into yet another drinking session; we had to celebrate didn’t we? Ron and Charlie were well chuffed. They’d never had much luck over the years and they’d always felt on the outside, but now we’ve all got a successful business, we were all on the same level.

The older you get, the quicker time goes, and the next five years flew by. We never really saw much of each other. Vinny and Steve got really close. Their property empire was massive, but Steve was still passionate about The Punch Bowl. I could totally understand that. If Tracy hadn’t have died in such tragic circumstances, then

I'd probably still be running it. Bunny helped Helen out with the baby and they done a lot together. Charlie was doing really well with the scooter shop; he still specialised in restoring old ones, but he was making most of his money selling new ones. Ron was doing alright. Vinny got out of the escort industry at the right time; the days of earning a fortune were over. It was a combination of the worst recession the country's seen, and the market being flooded with Eastern Europeans, mainly Romanians.

Me and Judy stayed in Brighton and we turned the shop into a specialist Mod clothing outlet. We done a lot of business online, but there was never any shortage of Mod enthusiasts popping in. A lot of them were friends I'd met over the years at different events. I was still a leading figure within the scene; one of the faces. As much as I loved the clothes and my scooter, it was always the music I liked most. I've always been a life-long fan of the *The Who*.

Back in the sixties, my bedroom walls were covered in newspaper clippings and pictures of *The Who*. I can remember sitting in front of the TV in my soaking wet Levis watching them on Ready Steady Go, with my Dad looking on in disbelief thinking they were a load of louts. He just didn't get it.

Me and Judy had done a lot of travelling; we'd seen all the Wonders of the World and she never did get me back to America. I felt a bit bad, but I just didn't fancy it and then I came up with a great idea. It was October 2012 and *The Who* were about to embark on a tour of North America. Now, me and Judy usually went to Spain for the winter months, so I said to her let's do a tour of America instead. She was over the moon, getting all lovey dovey and thinking was really considerate, then I hit her with the bombshell that we'd be meeting up with Wolfy and following *The Who*'s tour. She soon changed her tune, but, like all good marriages, we come to a compromise and I agreed to only see eight of their shows while I let her pick a holiday in the sun at the end; somewhere in the Caribbean. It was all booked and we flew out at the end of November. The shows were great; Wolfy managed to get me a back stage pass and I finally got to meet Pete and Roger. I really liked the Americans. We met a lot of Judy's old friends from when she used to live there. We saw the last show at the end of February then flew over to St Lucia. It was a beautiful Island. We spent the first week relaxing on the beach then we hired a car and explored the sights. There weren't much to see, to be honest, but we found some nice little restaurants away from the crowds. We found a nice fish restaurant near a little bay got a cold beer and sat outside in the shade waiting for our lobster to be served. Twenty minutes later we could hear the cook singing as he brought it out. I took my sunglasses off, looked up, and couldn't believe what I saw.

"Fuck me. Rudy"!

"I not Rudy. I is Bob".

"Oh my God. Rudy"!

He quickly put the lobster on the table and pulled up a chair.

"Listen, man. Keep it down. Meet me in The Blue Oyster Bar tonight. I'll explain".

We were in total shock. It had been about fifteen years since he'd disappeared and we all thought he was dead. I didn't know whether to give him a hug or knock him out. We met him at The Blue Oyster Bar and he took us in a jeep up to his house in the hills. It was fantastic – it had great views of the bay. We sat out on the veranda while he got us some drinks.

"So Jim, how you doing my man? And you, Judy? You looking fine".

"We're alright. So what's your story"?

"Look, man, before I start, if my woman comes home, I'm

Bob. Alright? And you know me from when I used to sing in a club in Birmingham".

"Yeah, ok. Whatever. So what 'appened to you the night Roger got shot"?

"It wasn't supposed to happen like that. Winston promised we'd just take the money".

"So you was there then"?

"Yeah, man. I was there".

"Do you realise the danger you could have put us all in"? asked Judy.

"Could have, Judy. Could have. None of you gave a shit about the danger I was already in. You all did a lot of talking about how you was going to cover your arses, but no-one considered my arse".

"You got yourself in the shit with Winston, not us", I told him.

"You got a short memory, man. The only reason Winston was after me is because of what we all done to his old man. We all had a part in that".

Judy looked at me.

"He's right Jim."

"Yes I right. That money we took was no-one's".

"It was the Russians", I said, still pissed at him for defending his actions.

"No, man; it belong to the lady they kill. If the Russians got heavy over the money, then Mr Big Shot, Jack Warren, had plenty. I listen, I hear what you say; he had about one hundred million. The only way Winston was letting me off the hook was if I could pay him off at least one million".

"There was five million there".

"I know man and he take it all. He give me just two hundred thousand".

"That was enough".

"It was nowhere near enough to stay in England, but enough

to start a new life over here. You got to look at it from my point of view, Jim".

Rudy was right: if I had been in his position, I would have done the same. Anyway, it was a long time ago and to be honest, I was just glad to see him.

"So what happen in the end"? He asked. "I left for here the next day".

"Well Jack got his daughter back, the Russians fucked off back home, and we all lived happily ever after".

"No come back from the police then"?

"No. It didn't take them long to sort it all out. They had it down to the Russians shooting Doreen's lot and they knew Roger was linked to Ray, so he survived and went to the Russians to sort it out and they shot him and went home. The one who came out on top was your mate, Winston".

"He no friend of mine, but we're cool now".

Judy tried to smooth things over,

"Well, it's all water under the bridge now and we've all moved on. This is a nice place you've got here".

"I love it. I never gonna leave".

"So, do you own the restaurant"?

"Yeah. Me and my wife".

"So, you're married as well? We gonna meet her then"?

"No, I'd rather you didn't. I have a good life here and I don't want to risk anything messing that up".

"So you're never coming home then"?

"Home"? He replied. "This is my home. I never classed England as home".

We stayed talking to Rudy for about an hour and then left. He had a good life and we promised not to tell anyone where he was, but to be honest I don't think anyone would have given a shit about him anyway. We got back to Brighton the second week of

March and it was freezing. I wish we'd stayed in the sun, but being away for over three months had knackered me out. I didn't plan on doing a lot in April and May because in June I was following *The Who* on their European leg of the tour.

June came around quick enough and here I am, sitting on my favourite bench. It's the fourteenth; the day before I set off for the O2 in London to see *The Who*. I'm sitting looking out to sea like I've done a hundred times before and assessing my life. The Jam once sang 'To Be Someone' must be a wonderful thing; a famous footballer, a rock singer or a big film star. Yes I think I would like that. Every kid thinks they would like that, but they don't see the price you have to pay for being a someone. I wasn't a stupid kid; I knew the odds of me being the next James Dean or Elvis Presley were pretty poor ,and I was only averagely intelligent, so I knew realistically I'd end up doing some crappy job like my old man. As a kid I really struggled with that thought. I thought I was the only one, but the truth is: most kids felt the same. I remember thinking just before I left school that I'd rather be a bank robber like Bonnie and Clyde than a dustman or warehouse worker. Alright, it was a stupid idea, but at least it weren't boring. It took me a while to realise life weren't about the job you do, but about what you done with your life after work and how you spent the money you earned. That's why Mod came just at the right time; me and my mates had jobs, we were living at home, and we had plenty of money to splash around. It gave us an identity, separating us from the older, boring generation. Our parents had different ideals and values to us; they had lived through the war, getting by on ration books and few luxuries. When the war was over they were just grateful to be alive, so doing a shit job, then coming home to a hot bath and a hot meal meant the world to them. I think a lot of parents were bitter and jealous of us and who can blame them? The war robbed them of their youth. Was the anger I got from my Dad justified? Did I act like a spoilt brat splashing cash about on clothes, scooters, and good times? Was I rubbing his nose in it? I think he felt I was. I think he thought I was saying "fuck you, old man! I'm better than you", and he was right. Being a Mod gave me pride and respect from my mates. It put to bed all them childhood fears of being a nobody.

I thought all parents were like mine and I felt united with my mates; it was us against the world. But I was wrong. I know that now, but at the time I was one seriously fucked up kid; the drugs and booze only fuelled my fucked-up state of mind. I felt let down by the arseholes at work, my family, and finally, my mates.

Then there were my eight years inside. Looking back, it was the best thing that happened to me. I got away from the booze and drugs that were adding to my confusion and, when I killed that ginger git and saved Jack Warren's life, I had celebrity status.

When I got out of prison, I discovered love – the love of a beautiful woman and, more importantly, a love for life that I so struggled with as a kid. I had it all; money, a club, shop and a beautiful wife. How did it go so wrong? Well, I can tell yer, it don't matter how happy and content you are, how settled and secure your life is, there's always some nasty cunt out there ready to piss on your parade. Only I could manage to piss off one of the nastiest bastard gangsters in the country, and that was Mike Warren. It took many years to shake him off, but I did it and life was a bed of roses again. Then there was Tracy dying. Up to the point of her death I thought I'd experienced the worst life had to throw at me, what with the police, gangsters and even getting chased by a fucking ghost, but none of that compared to the hammer blow to my heart I felt the night I walked into that hospital and was told she was dead. After her death, I slipped into a depression like no other. People kept telling me to remember the good times, but all I kept doing was going over the worst times. I could feel my life ebbing away before Judy came along and turned it all around. She said life is all about chapters and she was right. At sixty-six, I feel I'm entering the final chapter of my life. I'm sort of confused, but not in a bad, fucked up way like when I was eighteen. I'm sitting here, looking forward to seeing *The Who* tomorrow night. I'll be going with a group of lads of various ages from twenty to sixty-eight. When I was fifteen, someone in their thirties was old, fifties was really old, and in their sixties, they were knocking on death's door. I'm sixty-six, for fuck's sake, and I don't feel any different. It's baffling. Mick Jagger and the rest of *The Stones* still can't get no satisfaction, Tina Turner can still crack a walnut with her thighs, Pete Townshend and Roger Daltry are still singing 'I hope I die before I get old', and they've all got a few years on me.

So, after all the years of pain, sorrow, joy, disappointment, many highs and too many lows, all in the pursuit of wanting to be someone, has it all been worth it? It's like Paul Weller sang, 'To Be Someone must be a wonderful thing'. Is it really?

Fucking right, it is. I wouldn't change it for the world. Tomorrow night when Roger Daltry screams out,

"Who the fuck are you"? I'll scream back,

"I'm Jimmy! Jimmy the Mod! Mod till I fucking die"!